LAURAN PAINE

Murder in Paradise

G.K. Hall & Co. • Thorndike, Maine

Copyright © Robert Hale Limited 1969

Published in 2000 by arrangement with Golden West Literary
Agency.

G.K. Hall Large Print Paperback Series.

The text of this Large Print edition is unabridged.
Other aspects of the book may vary from the original edition.

Set in 16 pt. Plantin.

Printed in the United States on permanent paper.

Library of Congress Cataloging-in-Publication Data

Paine, Lauran.
    Murder in paradise / Lauran Paine.
        p.   cm.
    Originally published: Murder in paradise / by Richard Dana.
London : R. Hale Ltd., c1969.
    ISBN 0-7838-8799-X (lg. print : sc : alk. paper)
    1. Impostors and imposture — Islands of the Pacific — Fiction.
2. Large type books.   I. Dana, Richard, 1916-   Murder in
paradise.   II. Title.
PS3566.A34 M85   2000
813'.54—dc21   99-052855

CONTENTS

CHAPTER ONE

A Commissioner is Murdered

Raratonga, Tahiti, Polynesia, Emeraldia compose only part of a lilting list of names as alien to the world's inhabitants as the way of life the people of those idyllic places live. Or did live until the twentieth century caught up with them.

That's not quite accurate because in some places the ways of life haven't changed, and even where the twentieth century did make changes, it was half gone before the innovations appeared, and it took another fifteen years before they were unreservedly accepted.

It wasn't the modernisation people balked at; the dusky native of the South Pacific Community — called 'Micronesia' for some obscure reason by sociologists — was too complacent by nature to do manually what some electrical gadget would do. Modernisation was fine; it brought not just electricity, but it also brought motor cars, radios, wristwatches, even television where reception was available, electric razors, all manner of means for making life less difficult.

Perhaps it was as old Commissioner A. F. H. Friday once said: "These people have never known hardship except for an occasional typhoon that uproots their villages, and even then they have a great *luau* while they are rebuilding, so even that's all sunlight and laughter. They don't work; they aren't exactly lazy, they've simply never had to work."

But they balked at one aspect of modernisation. They deplored the sociologists who came to assist them in ordering their lives. Despite the earnestness of these well-intentioned people, the so-called 'Micronesians' detested them, but they were a kindly people, given to partying at the slightest pretext, drinking, singing, making love, so they simply admonished the sociologists.

No one could remember the last killing on Emeraldia nor when the last war-canoe had been launched against some other island. There had never been many hotheads because it was considered the height of personal degradation to show lack of total self-control. A person also 'lost face' in the Oriental manner by showing anger. After all, the world of Polynesians was midway between East and West; its shores had been touched as much by the culture of one as by the culture of the other. Frank Chang said with a wink, that if Kipling had just travelled a bit more he'd have seen that, in fact, East and West *do* meet, and blend rather well.

But, supposedly, the natives just were not a warlike people. Anyone living in Polynesia — or 'Micronesia' — could attest to that. They loved jokes and laughter, feasting and dancing, wearing flowers in their hair and moonlight swimming, drinking and drum-beating, but they were neither warlike nor easy to anger, so, regardless of what sociologists said and wrote, the plain fact was simply that the handsome native people were extremely tolerant, kindly, generous and good-natured.

There was no real reason for them ever to have been otherwise. They'd never had to defend their islands which were surrounded by thousands of miles of blue-green ocean. They'd never had to struggle for food; in 'Micronesia' every bush provided something, every tree, the grasses which were grazed, the seas, even the tropical air where varieties of plump birds flew. For a thousand years and longer these people in their blissful world of eternal sunshine, warm tropical rains, beautiful islands, bountiful sources of sustenance had never been forced to do anything they didn't want to do, so if they had ever possessed aggressiveness, it had long, long ago been winnowed out of them.

Sociologists irritated them. They were perfectly willing to welcome visitors to their islands. They were pleased when outlanders came to stay, living along the ivory-sand beaches. They accepted each new innovation modernisation provided, but they laughed at so-called 'civilisation', which they didn't need, and they frowned in annoyance at the people who came out of this 'civilisation' to study them, their ways of life, even their personal habits.

Eventually the islanders who disliked this invasion of privacy most simply packed up and went over to the far side of their island, or went deep into the tropical heartland to some village that adhered to the Old Way, or maybe filled a canoe with their brood and headed for some place, like Emeraldia, where civilization had been kept at bay by the former Commissioner, A. F. H. Friday, who had no authority, actually, since the islands were now autonomous, but who nevertheless gave pretty rough dictums on who could, and who could not, step foot on Emeraldia.

When the island had been a colony Commissioner Friday had come perilously close to being removed, relieved, and replaced, upon several occasions, but the two most notable circumstances involved the zealous Methodist Mission which he'd steadfastly refused to permit to set foot upon Emeraldia, causing quite a stir, and the time he threatened to personally escort an Indonesian premier to the dock and boot him off Emeraldia — using native supporters to offset the Premier's numerous entourage — unless His Excellency got his trouble-making party out of Ibehlin — Emeraldia's capital city; in fact, Emeraldia's *only* city — before sunset.

In both cases repercussions spread like ripples on a lake, both far and wide. The Methodists accused A. F. H. Friday of encouraging bare-breasted natives to live in iniquity, when, as a matter of fact, the natives had never needed any such encouragement. As for the Premier, he shook his carved-ivory baton and warned Commissioner Friday that his country had the fifth largest army in the world, capable of redressing all affronts to Indonesia's redoubtable *bungs*.

Friday had blandly said in rebuttal that if His Excellency wished to send his fifth strongest army in the world across the South Pacific, Friday would in turn send his first most beautiful girls in the world to meet it.

As for the Methodists, Friday had simply said, "Come back any time, ladies and gentlemen; we of Emeraldia will be pleased to supply each and all of you, *ladies* and gentlemen, with the native attire, which is a sort of printed diaper and nothing else, and when you will be perfectly at liberty to go among the people teaching your variety of Christianity. If the people like it, fine, if they laugh at it, I will sympathise with you because I was born, baptised and reared as one of you."

Outraged churchmen accused Commissioner Friday of heresy, apostasy, blasphemy, every denunciatory term dear to the heart of The Faithful, which caused scarcely a ripple in Polynesia although in several capitals of the civilised world there were murmurs of disenchantment about Friday's conduct; but he was never re-

11

moved as Commissioner of Emeraldia, and subsequently, when autonomy came, he was voted Chief Executive by a unanimous and overwhelming majority of natives. Of course this magnificent triumph was followed by a three-day orgy of drinking, singing, dancing, flower-weaving, feasting by torchlight, and unfortunately at the end of it, by the murder of Commissioner A. F. H. Friday.

Frank Chang, the late Commissioner's close friend, unerring supporter, and who owned the warehouses along Ibehlin's waterfront which he operated in conjunction with his export-import business, spoke for the majority of Emeraldians when he told a British newsman he frankly could not understand why anyone would murder Commissioner Friday, and that furthermore, after nearly fifty years of the old man's benevolent despotism, he had no idea what would now ensue.

Not that he anticipated trouble; the Emeraldians were too overwhelmed with sadness at the passing of their great protector, and besides, no one had any idea why Friday had been killed, let alone had any suspicions about who had murdered him.

"He was lying in bed looking very peaceful," Chang reported. "The servants at Government House thought he'd overslept and peeled back the bedclothes when they tried to awaken him. And there it was — the bullet-hole in the centre of his chest."

For a few weeks there was a vacuum. Where at one time elements of a foreign officialdom would have sprang to action, now there was an uneasy stir because, with autonomy, had gone tacit independence. No one was quite certain who had the authority, or if anyone had, to launch an investigation.

On Tahiti an elegant French official merely said, "Well; Emeraldia has been a smuggler's paradise for years. Perhaps Monsieur Friday became too greedy."

An American in Honolulu was less objective. He passed the murder off as being too far from Hawaii to be of much concern, and in any case Emeraldia was such a backward place almost any change would be for the better.

From Djarkata came a triumphant cry from the Premier to the effect that all men of power must learn that the Pacific Ocean was an Indonesian lake and those who struggled against destiny would perish even as A. F. H. Friday had perished.

That of course caused speculation that the sensitive Premier'd had a hand in the killing, but Frank Chang was disinclined to credit any such thing. "For one thing," he told Alan Barton, who freelanced for a number of British and American news services, "the Premier is just barely keeping his head above water in Indonesia; he wouldn't do anything like this because it could give his opposition all the excuse it needs to sink him permanently. For another

13

thing, the Premier isn't all that thin-skinned despite what people believe. I was with him during his visit to Emeraldia; he knew he was going to be invited to leave and it amused him more than angered him. He told me he was sure it would be to his credit in Asia where he wishes to be known as the champion of the masses, because Emeraldia is thought in those areas to be part of the Western sphere. Finally, he liked the idea of causing trouble this close to the U.S. mainland. No, I don't think the Premier had a hand in Commissioner Friday's killing."

Alan Barton's predictable rejoinder was, "Then who *did* have a hand in it?"

Frank Chang's equally as predictable answer was, "I wish I knew."

That was where the matter stood three weeks after Friday's death, during which there was a prolonged period of mourning, an enormous funeral during which time the Commissioner's effects were all bundled up and sent to London to his next-of-kin, a distant nephew named Ford Courtland, and Government House — which was a rambling bungalow with a corrugated tin roof and a gallery running completely around the place to provide dead-air space for cooling the rooms — stood empty and forlorn, as though with Commissioner Friday's passing an era had come to a close.

Perhaps it had, for as Frank Chang said to Alan Barton one soft moonlighted night on the dock out front of his warehouses, "We've never had any government here; never needed one. The Commissioner handled everything even after he no longer drew pay; taxes, levies, disbursements; he even sat as judge. The rest of us believed in him, and anyway, there was the matter of making a living." Frank flipped a cigarette into the oily sea at his feet. "I suppose that wasn't very enlightened, was it? But it worked, and I'm afraid of what will happen now."

CHAPTER TWO

A Visitor

Frank Chang's father — so rumour had it — had been an American sailor briefly stationed on Emeraldia during the Second War. His mother, dead seven years now, had been a fragile Chinese girl named Chang.

Frank was a handsome man, tall, lean, black-eyed but only distantly Oriental in appearance. He'd been educated in Hawaii. He'd also travelled extensively in America but had not liked it. He'd once told Commissioner Friday the States was a great jumble of noise and smells and frantic activity that overwhelmed a person, bewildered them, and, at least in Frank's case, finally, repelled one. He did not mention his reason for going there — To find his father. He'd been unsuccessful at it, which may have been for the best anyway.

The evening before The Airplane Incident while Frank and Alan Barton were at the bar of Mama Kameha's cafe — Ibehlin's only restaurant — Frank said, "I suppose the trouble is that living in a place like Emeraldia, one begins to believe in some kind of immutable immortality. Hell; it just never crossed my mind anything could ever happen to the Commissioner.

16

And yet he had to be at least sixty-five years old." Frank was down in the dumps that evening; every time he got to drinking and thinking of the departed Commissioner he got that way.

"On the other hand there was no reason for murder, Alan. Emeraldia's off the path of this tiresome East-West confrontation. We have nothing they'd want; we're too small, too poor."

"My guess," said Barton, "is that it was a personal thing, Frank."

Chang's head came up, his brows knit. "How?" he asked. "Why? What for? Alan, the Commissioner was a poor man. I know that for a fact. Since we became free he hadn't got a cent of pay and he only took a couple of hundred dollars a month for salary from the tax fund. Anyone who knew him at all, knew he didn't have anything."

"Do you remember what the Frenchman said, over on Tahiti?"

Frank made a gesture. "Those Frenchmen," he said contemptuously. "If they aren't drinking wine they're losing wars. That remark about the Commissioner dabbling in smuggling was ridiculous. Smugglers have never needed Emeraldia. Tahiti is more centralised for their traffic, or even Hawaii. Besides, if that Frenchman had known the Commissioner he'd never have implied dishonesty."

"All right," Barton conceded, winking at obese Mama Kameha for refills. "Then

17

someone had a personal grudge. Someone here on the island. Perhaps someone off one of the little tramp ships that anchor here from time to time."

Frank shook his head. "No ships were docked that week, Alan, you ought to know that. As for someone on the island — who?"

Barton had no more idea now, a month after the murder, than he'd had the day after. He sipped his refilled glass, considered the indifferently turning great fan above the bar, and finally put his glass down as Chang said, "I'll tell you what I think, Alan. I think we're never going to know who killed the Commissioner, nor why. No one heard the gunshot. No one has yet come up with a single sound reason. We buried him all the same, and that's how mysteries come to life. Time passes, everyone sits around sipping mango juice and rum advancing theories, and after a while that's the end of it. Presto! A genuine island mystery." Frank raised his glass. "To Commissioner Alfred Frederick Harold Friday!"

The very next morning they had The Airplane Incident.

Alan was at his typewriter winding up a ten-thousand-word article that verbally squeezed every last drop of juice out of the murder of Commissioner Friday. There was no doubt of it, the thing was becoming *passé*. In this day and age unsolved murders were too frequent to hold the limelight very long, but Alan had to get one more cheque out of the affair because otherwise there just was nothing of newsworthy interest in his corner of 'Micronesia' at the time.

Frank Chang was in a copra shed where the hulls were sliced by murderous great knives, placed on conveyor belts and the halves were then sent out to be placed on sticky trays in hot sunlight to dry. A copra shed — or even a drying area out in the open air — had a very unique aroma. It was musty and sticky and somehow sweet-smelling in the same way that tobacco and spiced sugar might be sweet-smelling.

Curing copra had a scent all its own. Frank was so accustomed to it he didn't even notice. Neither did the grinning, sweaty natives with the shiny knives who worked for him.

He was standing back by the rattling motor that worked the conveyor belt when a more distinct sound eventually caught his attention. Several of the natives at their long slicing table happily put down their knives and went to the doorless opening to look skyward. Aircraft were not novelties exactly, but low-flying small ones certainly were rare over Emeraldia.

Frank went to join his blithe workmen while the conveyor belt clanked emptily along and the wheezing old motor coughed and panted, gasped and wheezed in the background.

There had, a quarter century earlier, been an emergency landing strip built out in the bush on Emeraldia, but jungle had long since obliterated it. In fact, there were trees growing out of the tarmac now that anywhere else in the world would have been at least a hundred years old to have reached the same girth and height.

Frank said to his copra-shed foreman that flyer up there had to possess more courage than common sense; he flew so low treetops bent from prop-wash. The foreman grinned in delighted approval of both Frank's observation and the daring of the pilot.

The airplane buzzed Ibehlin driving everyone into the single roadway. It rattled windows in Alan Barton's bungalow and he too ran outside. When the pilot appeared satisfied he'd roused everyone he stood his underslung little aircraft on its tail, walked straight up the sky for a mile or so, then levelled out, cut his engine and seemed to hang motionless while something crooked and lumpy dropped earthward.

Frank's foreman said cheerfully, "Japanee bomb!"

Frank was too surprised to pay much attention to that, or the other shrieks either, for a parachute opened and the crooked, lumpy thing straightened out to become a man floating to earth above the wide beach. It was obvious, finally, why all the aerobatics had preceded the drop. Pilot and parachutist wanted help on hand when the skyborne visitor hit the ground, or the treetops, which was more likely.

Frank ran for his Land-Rover, kicked it to life and went lurching away in the direction of that broad beach. Unless the parachutist was very skilled he would drop in the sea, in which case, weighted as he was, he would either be dragged under or, if a wind drove him far enough out, sharks would finish him.

Alan Barton, whose bungalow overlooked the white sand and emerald surf, had merely to slip into his sandals and lope through the palms to arrive down there first. The parachutist saw him and waved. Alan waved back. Frank came zig-zagging along while the skyman was still well above the treetops, and looked for the little aircraft. It was a speck in the sun heading towards one of the Leeward group.

Alan came to the side of the Land-Rover, shaded his eyes, and said, "Risky business, that."

Frank had a more colourful suggestion. "Damned fool's got to be out of his head. He's got one chance out of five of hitting the beach."

They craned their necks while the descending man spilled air from his parachute to prevent a seaward drift. He was obviously experienced at this sort of thing.

When he was a few yards above treetop-level in the breathless silence he called downward, his voice sounding a little eerie coming out of the sky like that.

"Thought I might get hung up. Sorry if I

caused a fuss. I'll manage now. Thanks for standing by."

He managed expertly, landing not thirty feet in front of the Land-Rover, taking one complete roll and coming upright on both feet at the end of it. He was a sandy-haired, grey-eyed, big-boned and tough-faced individual who smiled easily, but he had an attitude or an aura about him that was not entirely easy-going despite his smile.

He gathered the parachute, held it to his stomach and walked over. "Ford Courtland," he said, offering his hand. After Frank and Alan had shaken it and introduced themselves Frank's black eyes narrowed. He'd been the one who'd sent Commissioner Friday's personal things away. The name Courtland meant something to him.

Courtland said, "Not the best jumping or landing conditions, but it cost too much, and I'd have had a three-day wait, to charter a boat to Emeraldia." He looked at the greeny bay, the lovely beach, the tropical bush to his right, then he grinned broader as he said, "I thought Emeraldia was modern. Well, what I meant was, most places have landing fields now, and regular boat-traffic. You fellows are pretty well isolated, aren't you?"

Alan said drily, "Some people like television and detergent soap, others don't, Mister Courtland."

The tough, confident grey eyes made their

slow, bold assessment, then Courtland said, "Mister Chang; that was a very thoughtful letter you sent along with my uncle's things. I got the feeling from it you thought a lot of him."

Frank nodded. "I did." He then said, "But if you came all the way from London about the Commissioner's death I'm afraid it'll prove a disappointment, Mister Courtland."

The sandy-headed, smiling stranger gazed a moment at Frank before he said, "As a matter of fact I've been living in California for the past couple of years, Mister Chang, so it wasn't really such a long flight. And as for my uncle's death," the big shoulders rose and fell, "the police ought to be able to fill me in, shouldn't they?"

Alan and Frank exchanged a look. "We have no police on Emeraldia," said Alan Barton. "Your uncle was the judge; when someone did something wrong, he'd get whoever wasn't busy that day to take a few friends and bring the culprit in. Apart from an occasional drunken wife-thumping, or someone making off with someone else's string of drying fish, we have no crime."

Courtland's smile faded as he listened, then he said, "Sounds a little like paradise, gentlemen. Well, if I buy all hands a round of drinks do you suppose I could cadge a ride into Ibehlin in the car?"

Frank pushed aside some copra sacks, some

23

tools and odds and ends to free the passenger's seat for his guest. Alan clambered into the back and had to perch on top of some small oil tins. There was no real reason for him to go along at all except that he was curious by nature and interested by profession.

Courtland asked about a place to stay. Frank Chang said Mama Kameha had rooms out the back of her bar, Courtland then asked about the island, and it was much easier for his escorts to talk on that subject; they knew Emeraldia very well and they liked it. There was excellent fishing, wild pigs in the interior for hunting, any number of very picturesque coastal villages on the rear side of the island where natives danced to music from Japanese transistor radios, and of course there was the languor and sunshine of the village — which was called either a city or town by everyone although it hardly qualified on either count, being only one long, broad, uneven dusty roadway with stores and houses on both sides.

Courtland seemed pleased, but Frank noticed how those smiling-tough grey eyes swept left and right missing nothing, making assessments, observing, only smiling on the surface. Frank was beginning to form some kind of opinion of the newcomer and it didn't quite square with the easy smile. Courtland wasn't any golden boy who dropped out of the sky for the love of it. He was a man of at least thirty-five with the scars of living in his rugged coun-

24

tenance. He didn't hop across the Pacific Ocean and sky-drop just because he loved adventure. Perhaps fifteen years earlier he might have been that kind, but not now.

Frank eased to a stop out front of Mama Kameha's tin-roofed establishment, offered Courtland a cigarette, held the match for him and said, "Alan and I have a drink or two at the bar here every night. We'd be pleased if you'd join us this evening, eh Alan?"

"Delighted."

Courtland smiled that easy smile of his. "I owe you a drink now, for bringing me in."

"I've got to get back to work," Frank said. "How about saving it for later?"

Courtland climbed out still clutching his balled-up parachute and looking huge in the baggy, lumpy jumpsuit. "Dinner too," he said. "I'll be waiting. Thanks awfully for welcoming me. It's very kind of you both."

He saluted casually turned and walked towards the tin-roofed building. Alan said, "That's about all the excitement I can stand in one day."

Frank grunted, turned his Land-Rover and headed back towards the copra sheds. He was reserving all judgement.

CHAPTER THREE

Some Doubts in Paradise

It took copra a long time to dry. Frank Chang operated on a shoestring, which meant he never warehoused very much copra at any one time, but he had to store some because the ships that came to Ibehlin Bay to take the crop off could neither carry very much, nor be depended upon to arrive on schedule.

It was a source of exasperation to Frank that his copra business was such a borderline enterprise. He'd erected the warehouses four years earlier. This was the first year his books would balance as a result of what he'd spent putting up the sheds.

He was explaining about all this to Ford Courtland when the latter evinced interest in Emeraldia's economy. Courtland had at that time been on the island four days and had been into the interior, had even hired a lad to show him the back of the island where the villages hugged coves and beaches. As Alan Barton had observed the evening of the third day, there was one thing which could undeniably be said of Ford Courtland — he was not a lazy individual.

Something else one could say for him: He could handle an alarming amount of liquor.

That fourth evening while he and Frank awaited Alan so they could have dinner, Frank gave up trying to match Courtland drink for drink. He didn't comment on the newcomer's capacity except to himself and if Courtland noticed that Frank played with his last drink instead of downing it, he did not comment either.

After Alan arrived Mama Kameha waddled in with their roast pork, yams, a salad made of avocados and papayas, and tea strong enough to hold its own with the strongest coffee.

Alan apologised for being late. There would be a boat in the harbour in the morning to take off mail. He'd had three finished articles to bundle up tonight because he hated rising early in the mornings.

Ford Courtland asked about the articles. One was on the enduring mystery of Commissioner Friday's murder. Of that one Alan said somewhat apologetically and honestly that he'd done the tale, not because he felt it would stimulate much interest at this late date, but because he needed some money. The other two articles had to do with fishing in the South Pacific, which was a sort of travelogue, while the third article, as Alan candidly stated, had to do with about the only other thing, native lore aside, which was of much interest to the rest of the world — the island-hopping proclivities of, first, the Japanese during the Second World War, then the equally as determined and infinitely more successful island-hopping of American forces pushing the Japanese back.

Courtland was politely interested. "Are you a scholar of the Pacific War?" he asked Alan.

The answer, as Frank Chang knew and as Alan admitted, was that Barton wasn't really a scholar of anything. He was a man who enjoyed life, whose needs were actually simple, but who was interested in just about everything around him. He laughed softly and said, "Hardly a scholar, Mister Courtland. Commissioner Friday was that. I'm just a person who has been to nearly all the islands and seen the old caves, stockades, airfields, bombed-out bunkers and overgrown old rusted tanks and trucks. It seems strange sometimes, Mister Courtland, to stand in the centre of an empty airfield and hear nothing but a trade-wind in the treetops, and think of the thousands upon thousands of men who were once there with all kinds of noisy machinery and ships and guns. It's like stepping back in time, finding everything as it should be — except no people. Nothing at all but perhaps an overgrown military cemetery."

Frank Chang winked at Courtland. "Alan's an incurable romanticist. But he's right about one thing — it can be a little spooky, standing in a Jap bunker sighting down a rusty gun barrel at a big mound of earth where the Americans once dug in, and not hear a sound."

Courtland nodded sympathetically. "Did the war reach Emeraldia?"

"Not really," said Frank. "There was a Japanese evacuation centre on the back of the island where it was hidden from the U.S. navy. They kept the wounded there until they could be taken back to Japan, but neither side ever shelled Emeraldia or fought over it. Near the end, when the Japs finally cleared out, a regiment of American marines landed." Frank jerked his head in the direction of the bar where Mama Kameha was serving drinks. "Ask her, she was here through the entire thing. She says the marines landed on a Wednesday, deployed on Thursday, swept completely across the island on Friday, returned the same way on Saturday, and were taken off on Sunday." Frank smiled. "That was the extent of Emeraldia's part in the war and there isn't even any mention of our island in the war histories. Hell of a note, eh?"

They all laughed. Mama Kameha came over to see if they needed anything and Frank told her what he'd been talking about. She nodded, her dusky, round, smooth face unsmiling in spite of the grins of the men. She said, "A person has a long time to think, in twenty-five years, so now while it's funny to you, I wonder whatever became of the *banzai*-boys who left a leg or arm here, or who never saw anything after they looked up at the treetops before blindness struck. You know, I been to Japan. It's a pretty crowded place. Not like Nebraska or Wisconsin. I been those places too; they take care of their heroes. In Japan there were no heroes and it's a pretty crowded place. Where does a blind man go to make a living for his little family, or where does he hop on one leg, or what factory wants him to operate a machine with one arm?"

The three men no longer smiled, but as Ford Courtland said, "Mama — who attacked whom in that stinking war?"

She nodded. "I know. In fact, I knew one of you would say that. I'm not blaming anyone; all I'm telling you is that in some ways it was a lot worse looking at the enemy wounded right here on this island than it was to hate and kill them as fighting men on some of the other islands. And all I got out of it was a sickness it took me five, ten years to get over. I never liked Japanese; they were bad here in the South Pacific for ever since I was a child." She leaned across the back of Frank Chang's chair and said quietly, "But you cry until there are no tears left when you hold one's hand in the underbrush while he tells you of little Iseki, six months old when he went away, and of little Iecho, his wife of two years who he loved very much. His belly is a pouch without half its entrails. They don't even put him in one of their tents. He dies in his sleep because at least they give him that much heroin or something."

Ford Courtland said, "Mama, there was never any such thing as a *good* war, not even the Crusades or the wars for independence, but never forget this: There have always been and always will be, *necessary* wars. The only people who can't see that or who won't believe it, are the people who will be conquered. That's the way the ball bounces. You and I as individual people don't have to like it nor even understand it — but we sure as hell have to live with it. How about another glass of that *sake,* it's the best I ever tasted."

Mama's brown eyes lingered for a long while upon Ford Courtland before she went after a fresh bottle. He afterwards made a self-conscious small smile and said, "Well, I put my foot in it I'm afraid. She didn't like that."

Alan wasn't convinced. "You'll get to know her. She doesn't carry grudges. She isn't offended when people have views different from her views. She's really very pleasant, good-humoured and kindly. Commissioner Friday thought the world of her."

Courtland looked at Alan. "Is that so? Was he on Emeraldia during the war too?"

Alan glanced at Frank as though for corroboration of his reply. "As I understand it, he was taken off by a Royal Navy corvette shortly after the attack on Pearl Harbor, and did not return until the mess was over. Is that right, Frank?"

Chang nodded, wiped his lips with a paper napkin, leaned back and fished for his cigarettes. He looked directly at Ford Courtland, "Didn't you see him during that time, or hear from him? I'd have thought he'd surely have

31

kept in touch with his kinsmen."

Courtland shook his head. "It wasn't that easy in those days. I was evacuated to Scotland along with a great horde of other youngsters. Didn't even hear from my parents for a number of months — until the blitz let up a bit. To tell you the truth I hadn't corresponded with my uncle in something like six or eight years prior to his death. I remember him only as a ruddy chap with a bristly moustache, piercing blue eyes, and a rumpled look, whose mouth was always pulled slightly to one side as though he were laughing ironically at life, or as though he knew something no one else knew, that was cruelly funny."

Alan opened the fresh bottle of *sake* when Mama Kameha brought it, filled their glasses in silence and afterwards said, "Tough old gentleman. He was the best chess player in the Pacific, I think. And he possessed the same capacity I notice in you, Mister Courtland: He could sit and drink half the night and never show it." Alan grinned. "Probably had a ruined liver as a result, but that was something else; he never complained. Fine old gentleman. Too bad he never married, but then I suppose that could be applied to a lot of us, eh?"

Courtland considered his glass of Japanese wine. "Rather permanent proposition, isn't it? Like dying, it's always there but I don't suppose there's any need to rush into it." He smiled. "We ought to be able to get a good discussion going on that topic. There are three of us sitting here who have survived the susceptible age and are still unmarried." He downed the *sake,* put the glass aside and leaned back in his chair. He was attired in a cream-coloured, short-sleeved shirt and light cotton trousers. They didn't look wrinkled enough to have been under his jump-suit so they must have been folded inside it some way when he'd landed four days earlier. His arms were finely haired and thick. He was a powerful man, physically, and his deep-set eyes looked out smilingly with all the confidence and poise of a man sure of himself in any position.

Frank finished his smoke, doused it and stretched. "Boat coming in the morning," he announced. "Twice a month I get up with the birds — when I can load copra and see what the mail brings." He grinned, his bright, very dark eyes showing wry humour. "I call it the Chang Export-Import Enterprises Ltd. which sounds elegant as all hell, but it's really just a mail-order business." Frank arose. "See you lads tomorrow, probably. If not during the day then here at Mama's tomorrow night. Good night."

They watched him depart and Courtland said, "Seems pretty decent."

Alan concurred. "He is. Genuine South Pacificer if there is such a term or such a hybrid. Mother was Chinese, father was an American sailor but Frank never knew him.

Doesn't even know what his father's name was. One of those things that happened a lot during the war."

"During any war," said Courtland.

"I suppose that's right. Frank's a good businessman. No quirks, very uncomplicated, predictable. I'd classify him as an all-round good man."

Courtland filled their glasses for the last time. "He seems to be the island's sole industry — copra and this export-import thing he mentioned."

"Pretty much," agreed Barton. "The natives sell fish — dried and otherwise — and they go to the outer islands to work sometimes, but you're right about Frank; without his sheds there'd be a lot less foreign exchange. You see, Emeraldia hasn't quite found its place in the twentieth century yet, and it may never find it because we're just outside the sea lanes, the air lanes, the tourist sphere." Alan smiled. "And personally, I like it just that way."

Courtland also smiled. "I've never been in a place quite like this before. It's a definite change."

They broke up shortly after this little discussion. Alan strolled homeward through the moonlit night following a well-worn dusty trail that skirted the waterfront, Chang's warehouses, his copra-sheds on the outskirts, and wound along a strip of palm-fringed white beach where the greeny surface of a timeless sea shimmered under starshine.

When he reached the bungalow he saw a glowing cigarette on his porch, and stopped a moment to consider this. Frank Chang's voice said softly, "Just me, Alan, come on up."

Alan resumed his way. "I thought you were deadbeat."

"You were supposed to think that. Care for a smoke?"

"No thanks."

"Sit down then. I've been wandering around thinking. I needed someone to sound out my ideas upon. Are you too tired?"

"Not tired at all after all that *sake*. What kind of ideas, Frank?"

CHAPTER FOUR

Arrival of the Doreen

"To start with," said Chang, "Courtland described his uncle exactly as the Commissioner looks in that public photograph they used every time he got into the newspapers."

"All right. What of that?"

"He said the Commissioner's mouth was pulled to one side like he was amused about something, Alan, but he didn't say why. You know as well as I do that the reason Mister Friday's mouth was quirked to one side was because of that scar that pulled his lips sideways."

"Okay. What are you trying to say, Frank?"

"He didn't know the Commissioner at all, Alan. When they touched up that photograph they eliminated the scar which made Mister Friday look just as Courtland described him — smiling — but with no obvious reason, which that scar made. 'You see?' "

Alan thought a moment while gazing down across the ghostly beach to the ocean. "He also said he hadn't seen the Commissioner since he was a kid — or something like that, Frank. Granting Mister Friday'd had that scar even in those days, a kid would very likely forget it wouldn't he? I mean, there was that damned war, London under attack, all that traumatic stuff."

Frank nodded gently as he listened, then he said, "Alan, let me ask you a question. If an uncle you barely knew got murdered in some god-forsaken speck in the South Pacific, and you were comfortably enjoying life in California, would you drop everything, climb into a parachute and risk your neck getting here to see what had happened to the old gentleman?"

Barton grunted. "Now I'll take that cigarette." For as long as it took Chang to offer the pack and to afterwards hold the light, Alan was silent. Finally, blowing out a grayish cloud he said, "I don't know. Probably not, but look at him, Frank; he's big and rough and adventuresome. I'll bet in his time there wasn't anything he wouldn't tackle."

"That's my point, Alan. *In his time* — but he's no trouble-hunting youngster any more. And watch him when he's sitting with you. He's as calm and shrewd and hard as they come."

"Wait a minute. Are you saying he's not the Commissioner's nephew?"

Frank tilted back the chair, put his feet upon the porch railing and blew out a big, fluttery sigh. "I don't know. There's something wrong, Alan, I can feel it. If he *is* Mister Friday's nephew, why doesn't he interrogate you or me, or the people who were servants in Government House when the Commissioner was killed; why just go tramping all over the island

37

like a tourist — why spend so much time pumping people the way he pumped us at dinner tonight, on Emeraldia's past and so forth? Why not get on the trail and keep on it? And if he's *not* Mister Friday's nephew, who is he and what's he up to?"

"How do you know he hasn't talked to the natives who were servants at Government House, Frank?"

"Hell; they went to work for me in the sheds, and they asked me who the stranger was. They'd have *known* who he was if he'd interrogated them."

Alan swept back a big lungful of smoke and let it out. The night was utterly still. It was past midnight now. Only the surf whispered and that was a fair distance from Barton's bungalow.

"You're getting me interested," said Barton. "There may be a story in this."

Chang snorted. "If there's a story involved I'd a damned sight rather read about it in a magazine than have to be some part of it, when there's also been a murder."

"He couldn't have had a hand in that, Frank, he wasn't on the island."

"You're that certain, are you? Alan, anyone can come here in the night from another island. We don't maintain any police patrol."

Barton, sympathetic up to this point, now dug in his heels. "Cut it out, Frank; you're making a regular pirate saga out of this:

Courtland — or whoever he is — glided to the coast under a full moon, hid his craft and slipped up to Government House, got inside, shot the Commissioner, then stealthily got back to his boat and sailed away — then came flying in a month later posing as the murdered man's nephew. It's too melodramatic, Frank. More than anything else, it lacks motive. You've got to have a motive."

Chang killed his cigarette. "There was a motive all right, chum. No one killed the Commissioner just to make sure his damned pistol was in working order. I don't pretend to have the foggiest idea what the motive was, but that lousy murderer had one all right." Frank arose. "Now I'll go home and let you get some sleep."

Alan arose smiling ruefully. "Decent of you. You come up here in the night and put all sorts of bees in my bonnet, then you say I'm to simply drop off to sleep. Good night, Frank."

"Good night."

That pewter moon crossed its star-spangled heavens, the silence got deeper and deeper until shortly before dawn, and Emeraldia lay beach-girt, dark green and ghostly in a curving far world of clear, warm water.

The nearest island was eighty miles to leeward. The sea-lanes lay off in that direction too, but not so far, and although there were airfields, to whose winged occupants eighty miles was next to nothing in either time or space, Emeraldia was still an insular, forgotten, drowsy place, with a reason for existing, perhaps, but not as far as the bustling, modern world was concerned.

Jacob Voermann the Dutch skipper of the island — hopping ship *Doreen*, had upon more than one occasion said it would suit him fine if Emeraldia developed one of those freak volcanoes that sometimes came to life on tropical islands, and sank the whole landmass beneath the sea; it was barely profitable to go there twice a month, and except for the subsidy one got for hauling international mail he would never point his bow towards Ibehlin Bay. As for the copra, aside from the smelling up the *Doreen*'s hold, he couldn't haul enough to make anyone any money.

There was an occasional passenger, and that kind of money was pure profit because he always made the eighty-mile run at night — which meant no meals for passengers, a pure saving if there ever was one — and also because, since he was going there anyway, and standing space on deck cost nothing, whatever he could gouge out of a passenger did a lot towards improving his ordinarily gruff and complaining nature.

Usually his passengers going to Emeraldia were returning natives who'd been working elsewhere. They paid very little. Now and again Chang or that writer-fellow came and went. They of course paid a little better. And upon one or two extremely rare occasions Captain

Voermann had hauled in a complete stranger. They paid the best.

But this was the first time he recalled ever having heard of a lone young educated, extremely attractive woman booking passage to Emeraldia, and he knew for a positive fact it was the first time he'd ever taken one there.

Ordinarily he'd have found some way to open a conversation with his passenger. This time though the passenger paid, asked where her quarters were, went into the cabin and remained there until shortly before dawn, when she appeared on deck to watch Emeraldia firm up out of the onward dawn, and of course Captain Voermann was himself snoring in his bunk most of that time, leaving the watch to his pair of Australian crewmen.

He did, however, stamp out upon deck for the first sighting of Emeraldia; he could have timed it like that without an alarm-clock after twenty-years on the same run, and he did finally strike up that conversation too, but there wasn't enough time to develop it into an expanding exchange of confidences even if the very handsome lady passenger had been willing, which she obviously was not, so in the end Captain Voermann simply stoked up his pipe, puffed stoically and when she asked the size of Emeraldia he said, "On the charts it says three miles long, two miles wide. These atolls are common. The only ones people live on are the ones with good water."

41

"Emeraldia has good water?"

"It has. Otherwise how could it also have villages and a town? Well, in the old days a few remittance people sat out on these little specks and drank themselves to death and no one cared at all. Since the war I don't think there are any more remittance people about, and if a man has to earn the money for his booze, he drinks less of it, eh?" Voermann laughed, blew smoke, watched the way the air bent it, turned and gazed at the pristine beach up ahead where tropical growth looked velvet black instead of darkest green.

"I'd go crazy on that island. Half the time I don't think they even know what month it is. It wasn't much when it was a colony with its own Commissioner, but since independence, or whatever it is these atolls have now, and the murder of old Friday, it's nothing but a pimple of a place."

"Does anyone know why the Commissioner was murdered?" the lovely woman asked quietly. "There was something about it in the Brisbane newspapers as I recall."

"There was indeed something in the newspapers, but that's all. I suppose old Friday caned one native too many or something like that. No one knows why he was killed as far as I know."

"Did you know him, Captain?"

"*Ja;* he was a devil at draughts and could drink like a camel. I knew him just right."

"How did he impress you?"

Captain Voermann turned and slowly inspected his passenger. It was his custom to be the interrogator, not the interrogated. Well, he was only a few minutes away from docking anyway, which was scarcely time to draw the woman out as to her business on Emeraldia — and besides she was the prettiest thing he'd ever hauled to Emeraldia or anywhere else — so he sucked on his pipe, shrugged to himself and said, "Tough old man, Miss. Honest, straightforward and tough." Voermann chuckled, recalling something he'd nearly forgot. "Once he got into it with some missionary people. They wanted him to make native women wear shirts or something to cover up. He refused. They accused him of being a nasty old man and he said he'd leave it up to the natives and the missionaries to work it out, but first the missionary people would have to live in the Emeraldia villages exactly as his natives did." Voermann turned. "Do you see what he meant?"

"I see, Captain. I've heard the story before."

"Oh. Well; you asked what kind of man he was. *That* kind. Honest, blunt. I never could understand why someone killed him, unless, as I've said, he put the lash to the wrong native or something like that."

"He didn't lash natives, Captain. That wasn't permitted in his day."

Captain Voermann turned, gazed fixedly at

his passenger for a stolid moment as though to imply that perhaps lashing wasn't permitted but it was damned well done, then he grunted as his two crewmen padded forward on bare feet to make ready for the docking.

It was by then sunup, Emeraldia was rising from its silken mists, off the *Doreen*'s starboard bow several cockleshell native canoes were already over the fishing shoals, and until *Doreen* lugged her way round the protective headland behind which lay Ibehlin Bay and the picturesque little village itself, the island looked as it must have appeared to the first seafarers who ever encountered it.

"A fairyland," she murmured. "It's like a drawing out of a child's book, Captain. What is that peculiar scent?"

"Drying coconuts, Miss. Copra. That's what I take back in the hold, after I send you ashore and hand over the mail." Voermann removed the pipe, discreetly spat over the side, replaced the pipe and said, "Fairyland it may be, Miss, but if I never had to come here again after today it would please me very much."

The docking was an event. Natives stood along the wharf watching in grinning silence. There were several non-natives also watching, and when the lovely woman appeared upon the bow those non-natives seemed suddenly glued to the ground.

Mama Kameha was there in a clean dress, with her frizzy, greying hair under the restraint of a broad yellow cloth band, her normally round, smooth, bronze smiling face as a blank stone. She had also seen the shapely woman on the *Doreen*'s deck. If she recalled ever before having seen such a visitor to Emeraldia it must have been so long ago she'd forgot because now she looked just as shocked as the three men standing over closer to the dockside warehouse where native workmen were already juggling the conveyor belt into place so they could start loading the *Doreen*'s gloomy holds.

CHAPTER FIVE

Alan's Lovely Visitor

The introductions were brief, and if anyone was genuinely sorry to see the beautiful woman arrive at Ibehlin it had to be Alan Barton. Her name was Kathleen Scott and she'd come to Emeraldia to write a series of articles for the Jenkins newspaper syndicate which, incidentally, was world-wide, although its offices and primary publications were in Britain.

The way she explained it that evening at supper when Frank and Alan and Ford were making her welcome official with a special meal, Jenkins Syndicate had what were termed 'Sunday supplements' to most of its metropolitan editions, and over the years articles had been featured on every known area under the sun. Editorially, the staff was about to start round again; that is, it was about to go through the encyclopedia starting with Abyssinia, Afghanistan, so forth, and rewrite its articles. Then, when the death of Commissioner Friday made the press teletypes, people began wondering where, exactly, a place called Emeraldia was.

"So here I am, gentlemen. Emeraldia's first female newsman."

Ford Courtland gave her a very masculine smile. "I've seen my share of newsmen, but never one I would frankly call pretty before."

Alan was interested but right then, whilst they were all together, he said very little. Later, when the dinner was over and he could tactfully do it, Alan took her for a stroll of the town, the docks, and over along the beautiful beach, and this gave him an opportunity to explain that he was a free-lance writer himself, that he had in fact that very day dispatched a lengthy resumé of the Friday affair to the syndicate for which she worked, supplementing it with a good deal of background material on Emeraldia.

As he reported to Frank Chang the next forenoon, she'd been interested, not the least condescending, which occasionally was the case between professional fulltime correspondents and free-lance contributors. "But while we were sitting on my porch admiring the sea, she offered me a cigarette and right at the moment, although I didn't notice, when she drew the packet from her pocket, she dropped a note." Frank waited until Alan dug the paper from a shirt-pocket then read it. It was more accurately only part of a note. The paper had been torn off at the top and all that remained were two lines written in the thick, strong scrawl of a man. It said '. . . the old man knew, therefore his killing had to follow. But be very careful.'

That was all; there was no signature. Frank

studied the paper with a dark scowl. "Knew what?" he said, handing the note back to Alan.

"Kathleen Scott could answer, I can't."

"Is she really a newspaper correspondent, Alan?"

Barton thought so. "She's done newspaper work, I can vouch for that, Frank. She uses the proper terminology, takes the proper approach and asks the right questions. Of course, these aren't necessarily the sole prerogatives of newspaper people."

Frank, standing beyond the clearing where his natives were sorting the copra trays, looked at the ground. "I was as close to Mister Friday as anyone, but that note doesn't help a bit."

"Perhaps, Frank, whatever it was he knew, he found out just before he was killed."

Chang moodily seemed to accept this possibility. He looked down towards the village where Miss Scott was settled in one of Mama Kameha's little cabins out back of the bar-restaurant. "My guess is that Courtland also knows. It's beginning to look to me as though you and I are the only ones who *don't* know, Alan."

"Know what? That's the crux. If the Commissioner got killed because *he* knew, I'd just as soon remain in ignorance."

Frank looked back. "Suppose these people get the idea that you *do* know, or that I know?"

Alan watched Frank's people making certain the sliced coconuts were face up to the hot sun.

They were a brown-skinned, handsome people with ebony hair and dark eyes. They also had startlingly white, perfect teeth and laughed often. While working they kept up a running fire of conversation in *patois* — a mixture of French, tribal or island dialects, and English — but mostly they either gossiped or joked. They were an easy, warm and friendly people, in many ways very childlike, very trusting, and happy. Aside from the natural beauty of the island, it was these delightful natives who were another reason why Alan Barton lived on Emeraldia. As he said now, "This might spoil things, Frank. It could turn out to be a pretty ugly business. I think we ought to get Courtland and the woman aside and put it to them point-blank. Otherwise if this drags on it won't get any better but it could very easily get worse."

They decided nothing, though, and when they parted, Frank to return to work in the sheds, Alan to head for his bungalow and re-examine the mail he'd received, the only thing that was different was their private knowledge that Commissioner Friday's murder had indeed marked an end to an era — or perhaps it hadn't really put an end, perhaps it had simply set free some forces the Commissioner had been able to keep in check while he lived.

If Kathleen Scott had an ulterior purpose in visiting Emeraldia she didn't give any inkling of it over the next two weeks of her stay. On the other hand, as Frank told Alan one night when they were strolling towards the north end of town after their usual supper at Mama Kameha's place, the very fact that she'd passed herself off as a newspaper reporter gave her an ideal excuse for all the long hikes she took into the interior, over to the far-side native fishing villages, and elsewhere.

"Gathering local material," said Alan, in agreement. "Well, of course she could be doing just that."

"I keep remembering the note," said Frank. "And she's not once asked me about Mister Friday. If she'd been curious I'd have wondered less, but there was the note, proving she knows something about Mister Friday we don't know, and yet she never mentions his name."

Of course, as Alan said, if that old war-surplus shortwave wireless up at Government House worked, they could make enquiries, not just about the lovely woman but also about Ford Courtland. But it didn't work, hadn't in fact worked for a year prior to the Commissioner's death and no one had ever considered it important enough to send out for new parts. Now of course they couldn't send out — the *Doreen*, their sole contact with the world, wouldn't return for another few weeks, and that would be the only way they could send for, and receive, new tubes and condensers for the transmitter. They couldn't even mail any letters. After discussing this briefly they parted that night agreeing that it was like living in a self-imposed vacuum.

Kathleen Scott visited Alan Barton's bungalow the following morning, cheerful and as pretty as a picture in a soft white blouse, tan hiking trousers and soft tan leather boots. She had her brown, wavy hair confined by a beige band that made her forehead seem wide and high. It also made her very lovely eyes the focal point when Alan studied her coming up on to his porch, where he normally worked in the mornings before it got so hot he retreated indoors.

He'd seen her with Courtland a half-dozen times down along the beach, walking and talking. He'd also seen her standing alone in soft starshine upon the wharf, different evenings, and no matter what the circumstances were, she was beautiful. He thought that, as he watched her approach his porch this morning.

She had to be about twenty-three or twenty-four years of age but by moonlight she looked sixteen and now, walking through the cool morning sunshine towards the bungalow, she looked a wholesome twenty. He had no idea of her background, her past life, her education or family, and he didn't really care about any of that. She was one of those women that when a man looked at her he was conscious of only two things — himself and her.

Her greeting was friendly, almost comradely, as though in sharing a profession they also

51

shared other things. Alan liked that approach; in fact, as he got her a chair and offered tea — which she declined — he couldn't think of very much about her he did not admire. She was a woman who exuded femininity. It would not be possible for a man to ever think of her in any other way. And yet she seemed so capable and knowledgeable Alan had no inclination to act protective towards her.

"I've tramped this island from one end to the other end," she told him, smiling. "I've seen the way they dry fish in the villages out back, I've been shown those stone idols no one knows anything about, and I've been over the site of the Japanese evacuation facility — all over-grown now with bushes and trees until the cemetery is almost obliterated. But I haven't visited Commissioner Friday's grave." She was looking up at Alan as she spoke. When she ceased speaking she still looked at him.

He caught hold of a chair, dropped astraddle of it and said, "It's on the little cleared knoll a hundred or so yards behind Government House. Any of the natives who've been guiding you certainly could have shown it to you."

"Of course, but that's not what I wanted, Alan." She turned to gaze out over the greeny sea. Barton's bungalow was ideally located for serenity, for beauty and solitude. She said quietly, "This is the most lovely spot on the entire island, Alan. I envy you." Then she smiled and became brisk again. "I want you to take me to his grave. You or Frank Chang, and he seems to avoid me. Maybe it's my imagination. In either case he's always so busy down there . . .'"

"You want someone to help you establish a mood, is that it?"

"Yes, that's it. I want someone who knew Commissioner Friday very well, to go up there and sit in the quiet shade and tell me all about him."

"I see. And how does that fit in with the rest of your assignment?"

"That will finish it, Alan. I've saved the Commissioner for the last. When I've got the background material on him then all I have to do is sit in my cabin at Mama Kameha's and make two typed drafts, the rough one and the finished one." She smiled.

"Ford Courtland's been to the grave a number of times," he told her.

"He didn't know the Commissioner. At least he didn't know him as you and Frank Chang did. He told me he hadn't even communicated with his uncle in something like eight or ten years."

"Did he tell you how he's coming along on his investigation of the murder?"

She shook her head, studied the railing in front of her, seemed uninterested. It appeared that Alan's bringing Ford Courtland into the conversation had sobered her, had taken away the sparkle, the smile, the lilting sound in her voice. She didn't speak for a while, heightening the impression that her mind had gone to sombre private reflections.

He interrupted the mood by saying, "I'll go up there with you, of course, only I think you ought to get Frank to go along. He and the Commissioner were very close."

"Officially?"

"That way too, yes, but, primarily, they were good friends; got on extremely well. Almost like father and son."

She looked up quickly. "Frank's half Chinese."

Alan, in the act of lighting a cigarette said drily, "Yes, I know. We're an awfully long way from any place that could be thought important, Kathleen. Emeraldia isn't any melting pot like Hawaii, nor is it any race-conscious country like Mainland China. People on Emeraldia have been happily blending for a long time. Hadn't you heard of the Spaniards who were shipwrecked here several hundred years ago, or the British pirates and French mutineers who settled down among the natives?"

"Yes of course. And I didn't mean to imply Frank's oriental streak was bad — I simply meant it might inhibit him from being compatible with an Englishman like Commissioner Friday."

"Frank was educated in the States, Kathleen. Commissioner Friday had lived nearly all his mature life in the South Pacific Community; the pair of them thought and acted very much alike — a sort of half-Yank, half-polyglot as it were. As for appearance, Frank doesn't look any more Chinese than I do."

She nodded. "I'm put in my place, Alan."

He grinned. "That wasn't my intention. Just helping out a bit with the background material." He stood up. "Come along then. I assume from your attire you wanted to go and visit the grave this morning before it gets too hot."

"Is it very much of an imposition?" she murmured, also arising.

Looking directly into her lovely eyes he slowly shook his head. "No imposition at all, but I still think we ought to stop by and take Frank along."

"He'd be too busy and that certainly *would* be an imposition."

It suddenly struck Alan that what Frank had said was true. This beautiful woman actually was avoiding Frank. It wasn't the other way around at all.

CHAPTER SIX

Marking Time

Almost anything one did on Emeraldia between five o'clock in the morning and high noon, was pleasant because the temperature never soared above sixty-five degrees fahrenheit, but from high noon until five o'clock the heat kept building up; not very gradually either, but instead with five to eight degree hourly increases until, with daylight still upon the island, it could get uncomfortably hot. Humidly so.

No one moved very much after noon. Of course it was always possible to get cool, which was a great blessing. The natives swam or went into the lush green interior where most of them had their huts, climbed into rope hammocks and were swayed to sleep in the shade by little trade-winds.

The outlanders usually sat on Mama Kameha's gallery — which, as with most buildings on the island, completely surrounded the place in order to keep cool shade on all sides of the structure, thus lowering all interior temperatures — sipping lemonade, drowsing, or, as today, talking and half-heartedly listening to the little transistor radio upon Mama Kameha's bar which tinnily but faithfully reproduced the sounds of Japanese music.

Ford Courtland said the illusion about a place like Emeraldia was an elemental and universal desire in people to escape to some place where the world passed on by, but the plain facts were simply that people did not actually want serenity; they might tire of the noise and frenzy of civilization, or even occasionally become pretty badly disillusioned and demoralized, but for the average person to have to spend any length of time in a place like Emeraldia would be the same as sentencing them to a prison term.

Frank Chang laughed as much because it amused him to hear a forthright opinion of his island paradise, as to find civilised people categorized in such a manner — by one of them — that they appeared not just frantic but also stupid.

He said, "Mister Courtland, if everyone really wanted to find a place like Emeraldia, where would the ones who couldn't be happy any other way, find what they were looking for?"

Courtland smiled at Frank, his hard eyes responding to the humour that was suddenly there on the porch with them. "There is always a place, Mister Chang. Only fools — notably black ones at the present time — think they can make the world over. Wise men set out to find the exact spot on earth that suits them, and settle there."

"Suppose there is no such spot?"

"But there is, Mister Chang; there is the exact location on earth for everyone. I know. I've criss-crossed this earth a dozen times."

Frank sat slouched, relaxed and pensively thoughtful. "You may be right at that. Emeraldia suits me just fine. I've been to most of the other places — America, Europe, Asia — I come back here. The question is, Mister Courtland, is it the man who shapes his land, or the land that shapes its people?"

"Both, and that's the secret, you see. To use an extreme example, an Eskimo would go crackers if he had to stay on Emeraldia. You would do the same if you had to stay at, say, Point Barrow. He is part and parcel of his environment, you are part and parcel of your environment. Commissioner Friday would have withered away had he returned to Britain after independence came for the island. Can you visualise him sitting in some gloomy hotel or club growing paler by the day?"

Frank nodded, glad the topic had finally got round to the Commissioner. "He *was* the environment hereabouts, Mister Courtland. The law, the faith, the philosophy, even the mystery." Frank turned dark eyes upon the other man. "Why did they kill him?"

"Who?"

"You tell me — you're the investigator, Mister Courtland."

The tough grey eyes turned hard and introspective, "I wish to hell I knew."

"You've been at it a month now. You certainly must know something."

Courtland lit a smoke, shook his head and tipped his cane-bottomed chair against the wall. "Everything I've dug up you could put on the head of a pin without any crowding. I found the hole where the bullet went into the floor. I dug it out but what the hell, I'm no ballistics expert; all I got is a gob of squashed lead. There was no gun. I've pumped those people who worked at Government House dry. They heard nothing, saw nothing, found nothing. Every time I start out, I find myself going round in the same damned circle again. Maybe Kathleen Scott is right; maybe every self-respecting island in the South Pacific is entitled to one good mystery. Tell me, Mister Chang, why you people don't bring in an outside detective?"

Frank said, "Who would pay him, Mister Courtland? I make a living here. Not a very fat one, but a living. Mama Kameha gets by about the same way. So does Alan Barton. The natives quit paying taxes when Mister Friday quit going round collecting them."

Courtland said quietly, "Do you know what you have here — anarchy."

Frank smiled.

"I'm serious. Not the kind that makes a lot of noise, runs amok with guns, accuses people of being one thing or another. You have the most primitive kind of anarchy known — no government at all. You people live like these islanders must have lived five hundred years ago."

"Is that so terrible?"

Courtland said, "Well, when someone is murdered it is bad, isn't it? No police, no money to hire them."

"And if we caught the murderer, Mister Courtland, would that change everything back again?" Frank shook his head answering his own question.

"You could set an example, Mister Chang. You could imprison him."

"We don't have a prison."

"Execute him then. Make it plain what happens to people who commit murder in your island community."

Frank sighed, listened a moment to the Japanese music then said, "He won't get away with it, Mister Courtland. We'll find out about him."

"How?" demanded the grey-eyed man and Frank looked directly at him.

"Someone will turn him up sooner or later. If not you then someone else. I'll tell you one thing; he didn't kill Mister Friday simply because he wanted to kill someone, and whatever his purpose, it will involve other people. It's like dropping a pebble in a pool — the ripples will spread and spread, touching a lot of other lives, until something he does or says, or someone he interferes with, will put the whole damned thing into proper context."

Courtland was wry. "You're quite a philosopher, Mister Chang."

"You are too, Mister Courtland. I thought that a while ago when you were evaluating our way of life on the island. You've lived a lot, been in many different places, understand how people function. The Commissioner was like that too; a very wise man." Frank glanced at his wristwatch. "Primitive or not, if I don't get back to the office and figure out the payroll, come Friday Mama Kameha will land on my back like a ton of bricks because that's when the people pay up with her."

He rose. "One question, Mister Courtland: Not *who* killed the Commissioner but *why?* That's got me more interested than who did it; almost anyone under the proper provocation will kill another person. You, me, even the natives. *Why* was an old man killed who had no money, who had turned his back on the twentieth century thirty-five years ago, and who didn't have an enemy? *Why?"*

Courtland also rose. He was wearing one of the blue denim shirts Mama Kameha carried on her shelves, standard attire on Emeraldia. His deep chest, wide shoulders and heavy arms filled out the cloth. "Mister Chang; you're a damned smart man."

"For a Chinese."

Courtland shook his head. "You're no more Chinese than I am, Mister Chang."

61

Frank softly smiled. "Okay. Go on."

"Any smart man in your boots would have some idea why Friday was killed."

They stood looking at one another. Frank finally shook his head. "But I don't, and that's a fact, Mister Courtland."

"You had access to all his files, all his correspondence, everything he did here on Emeraldia."

"True," said Frank. "And believe me, there wasn't a damned thing. Nothing. In fact, if you like I'll give you the files I stored in my back room from Government House and you can look through the lot. I've removed nothing."

Courtland made an impatient gesture. "Then he must have said something some time in an unguarded moment. I'll tell you one thing — Friday knew why he was killed. He may have seen it coming, he may not have, but when that final moment came, he knew. Now, when something that serious is on a man's mind, he isn't likely to keep it all to himself."

Frank was nodding before Courtland finished speaking because he had long ago been over this same ground. But he had drawn a blank then, and he drew one now. "I can give you the files. I can describe every situation we were involved in for the past half dozen years, Mister Courtland. There was no dope involved, no international espionage, not even any penny-graft."

Courtland said harshly, "That doesn't make

sense does it?" and Frank agreed that it didn't, but he was convincing. The reason he could be so convincing was because he was telling the absolute truth.

Courtland finally said, "Maybe I'll take you up on looking at these files one of these days. Thanks for the offer."

Frank walked back to his empty sheds. It was midafternoon and breathless even in the shade. He got a drink of water, wandered through the buildings to see that everything was as it should have been, then forced himself to enter the stifling little office and go to work on the payroll.

It wasn't much of a job, actually. Where all other businesses had to keep separate records — one for inland revenue filings, one for welfare deductions, another for depreciation, for overhead, for insurance, Frank Chang kept only the sketchiest kind of books for himself and paid in net amounts the exact wages he agreed to pay.

The weekend bookkeeping also kept him enlightened on practically a day-to-day basis respecting his net worth. It might have been a very gratifying system for most businessmen but for Frank whose net worth was considerably less than everyone thought, it was only a sobering method of seeing himself as he actually was — a shoestring entrepreneur on a forgotten atoll in the middle of the South Pacific Ocean.

He was more philosophical than Ford

Courtland knew. When he finished with the payroll, had all the little envelopes properly filled with cash and designated with the correct names, he strolled out among the drying trays, felt the faint overhead breeze, went down to the dock and let the scent of sea and sand and humid earth lull him for perhaps the millionth time into believing it was all worthwhile.

And of course Courtland — or whatever his name was — hadn't been wrong on Mama Kameha's verandah; each person was part and parcel of some appropriate environment. And he'd been right in another sense; Frank Chang was no more Chinese than Ford Courtland was. He'd known plenty of Asiatics; he didn't think nor react as they did. He didn't believe as Americans believed either, so of course that left him an Emeraldian.

Well hell, there were worse things. He lit a smoke and grinned at the greeny sea. He couldn't think right at the moment what things were worse, actually, than being an island-bound copra and import-export pedlar, but undoubtedly there *were* worse things.

A murderer, for instance, was worse.

That was one thing all environments seemed to share in common; condemnation of murderers. He turned to glance past the town back up towards the slight hill where empty and decaying Government House stood. Courtland was a shrewd, smart man. He'd been on the island more than a month now and unless he was deliberately taking everyone in, didn't know any more about who'd killed the Commissioner now, than when he'd first dropped from the sky.

Perhaps a professional detective would have solved that mystery long ago, but none had come, and even if one had, as he'd said to Courtland, who could have paid him?

On the other hand, Frank was convinced that what he'd told Courtland was the truth: Someday, someone was going to do or say something that would point to a killer and his reason for killing.

Frank flipped the smoke into the water and turned to go back to his bungalow which was to one side of his drying area — upwind.

Of course Courtland knew *something* or he wouldn't be on the island, so, having got no further must be more frustrating than Frank could imagine.

CHAPTER SEVEN

An Alien Sail

The section of the site where Government House stood had doubtless been in accord with some directive dictated a century earlier when men with a view towards maintaining the prestige of empire had seldom overlooked having the residences of governing officials established on lofty ground, even in an insignificant place such as Emeraldia where Government House had been built of local bamboo, hardwood logs, with a most unseemly corrugated metal roof that showed rust enough to detract from prestige, and had eventually decayed into what was a somewhat oversized but quite comfortable great bungalow.

Commissioner Friday had wielded a lusty axe and mattock. During his tenure the creepers had been kept within bounds, tree-suckers, those plagued innocuous little shoots that came springing out of the earth a hundred yards from the parent tree, had been felled with a savage blow, not to mention the more seductively fragrant mimosa, frangipani, and honeysuckle, the latter having been imported by some homesick commissioner's lady back about the turn of the century, and which had proliferated to such an extent since that time that it was now all over the island.

Commissioner Friday had never liked honeysuckle. "Damned stuff smells like one of those gardens back home," he once complained to Frank Chang, "where limpid ladies sit round mooning over lovers, instead of getting up off their great pink hams and scrubbing the woodwork!"

Alan Barton regaled Kathleen Scott with that story as they made their way along the path behind Government House to the slightly higher knoll where Commissioner Friday now lay. She thought it was delightful. She also wondered aloud why he'd never married. Alan's reply to that was succinct.

"Pretty difficult getting someone to spend their life on Emeraldia unless they are specifically suited for it. Besides, the old boy was something of a misogynist."

"Is that the grave?"

It was. There was a lovely little pagan altar built by grieving natives where someone came very often and placed fresh flowers. There was a little Japanese iron dragon for incense and over it all was a small roof made from a filched length of the corrugated metal from the roof of Government House.

The grave lay at the base of the stone and teakwood altar. Cement, which was very rare on Emeraldia — it turned to stone in the moist air — had been expertly formed and poured.

There was even a brass plaque which Kathleen studied then lifted blue eyes to examine the face of her companion.

"Your idea?"

Alan shook his head. "Frank's and Mama Kameha's and mine. Everyone chipped in, had the plaque made in Auckland and sent out on Voermann's boat."

She pulled back, glanced slowly around this small, quiet, slightly isolated little shrine where golden sunlight came through green leaves, and said softly, "I can almost know him here, Alan; can almost catch the essence of the kind of man he was." She smiled. "I hope I have — not as many friends because I won't have when I die — but the *kind* of friends he had." She touched the dew-fresh flowers. "An hour old."

Alan smiled. "The natives do that. You see Mister Friday wasn't a very complicated man; educated and wise, yes, but simple too. The natives knew exactly how he would react to things. They thought he was exactly as they were. He was their priest, physician, friend, even their sanitation engineer a time or two when mild epidemics broke out."

"It's a wonder they didn't try to avenge him, Alan."

"Against whom?"

Kathleen's lovely soft eyes lifted again, clung to Barton's face. "Surely they must have some idea who killed him."

Alan smiled tightly. "You've been pumping

68

them dry for days now. You know perfectly well they have no inkling who killed him."

She flushed, looked at the plaque and said, "Have you?"

He was still annoyed. He did not care much for deceit. "No. If you'd asked straight out I'd have told you the same way what I know about it — nothing. He was lying in bed, perhaps asleep, perhaps not; someone came into the room and shot him through the heart. I don't even know whether he passed from this life to the next one knowingly. If you'd like I'll show you the room where it happened."

"No thanks, I've already seen it. Alan; did he and Frank Chang have business ventures together?"

None that Alan knew of, but as he explained, he and the Commissioner, while good friends, were not all that close. "He considered me as something of a late-comer — an interloper as he'd have put it. Frank grew up here. His mother is buried here. He was gone for a few years but he and the Commissioner were even closer when he returned. I used to listen to them talk of an evening; they had pretty much identical views of the world away from Emeraldia. But as for business dealings together — no, I'd be willing to stake money on it that they didn't."

"Was the Commissioner here when the Japanese set up that hospital in the bush?"

"No. He'd been taken off months before."

"Then he never saw the Japanese?"

Alan lit a smoke, offered her one, got a refusal and went back to sit upon a sawn log that formed part of the little low fence that encircled this hallowed place. "Once when we were playing chess the Commissioner told me of meeting three Japanese who came to decorate the graves where they buried the ones who died before they could be taken back to Japan. He said one of those men had been the administrative officer. The other two had been surgeons. He told me that he and some of the natives used to keep the jungle out of the cemetery and keep the graves weeded and neat. The natives didn't like it; they hadn't liked the Japanese. The Commissioner said the old Japanese administrative officer was grateful. His own son was buried there. He'd wanted to send him back home for a proper burial but at that time the empire was falling apart, Jap airplanes couldn't always get through, and because it was so hot and all, the officer'd had to bury his son here. Commissioner Friday had those three Japanese at Government House for a week, until a boat came to take them off. He said although he didn't much care for Japanese, those three were middle-aged men like himself, and they sat a lot and talked, and he came to feel very close to them. So I suppose you could say, indirectly at any rate, that the Commissioner knew some of the Japanese who were on Emeraldia back during that war."

"Did he by any chance mention their names?"

Alan blew smoke and shook his head. "You want to detail your story too well. It will be boring if you do that. Anyway, he didn't mention any names even if he recalled them." Alan killed the cigarette. "Let it stand like that; it'll give more pathos to the story."

She said, staring at the grave, "I suppose one could, by going to Tokyo, dig up the names of the men who were stationed here, and trace them down in Japan." Then she looked up, saw Alan's faint frown and said, "Of course you're right. It would be better the other way; let my readers feel the pathos, as you say." She arose from the kneeling position she'd taken while he'd been telling about the Commissioner's recital, brushed a hand lightly across the little teakwood altar and smiled at the flowers. "I think I know him well enough to write about him now, Alan. Lean, forthright, practical, protective, somewhat introspective. Does that about cover him?"

Alan thought it did. "Add understanding," he told her. "He didn't really look it though, tall and saturnine as he was, but he had a knack for looking straight down into your soul. I thought the day we buried him up here, that there probably never were very many of his particular type at any one time in history, but at least in this part of the world when he passed on, so did the last of his kind."

Kathleen walked slowly across the little shady place with its cathedral sunbeams filtering down through treetops and said, "Didn't it ever seem odd to you that he never married?"

Alan arose and faced her. "Not really." He smiled crookedly. "You might be putting that question to the wrong bird anyway because I'm a confirmed bachelor too. Like Frank. Anyway, the Commissioner had a family; everyone on Emeraldia was part of it. He'd scold me for drinking too much just as quickly as he'd scold a native girl for spending the night on the beach with some boy."

"But the love, Alan, the affection . . ." She let the words trail off and nodded at him. "I understand. It was a thoughtless thing for me to say, wasn't it? He had the love, didn't he?"

"He had it, Kathleen, and to spare." Alan waited until she'd stepped over the sawn log then turned to follow along. "Now do you think you've captured the essence?"

"I think so. But it'll be a hard characterization won't it?"

They strolled back to Government House where the vines were already beginning to encroach. The veranda was shadowy and cool. Where trees had been allowed to flourish they cast shade. It was the drowsy time of day — high noon — and she stood upon the front gallery gazing down towards the town, a half mile and more onward, then farther out where the greeny sea heaved and rolled. The wharf looked fragile and it actually was, but that jutting headland to her right sheltered the little bay from storms. He explained that this was why Ibehlin had been founded in the first place.

"It's a natural harbour. Small of course, by most standards, but adequate. Typhoons that start in the China Sea go through the slot, which is what they call the southerly sealanes, and the backwash breaks against that headland. I've seen fishermen out there in their fragile canoes when the sky was as black as death, and hardly a groundswell ever reaches them in the bay."

"It's so — peaceful," she said. "So tranquil, Alan."

He smiled at her profile. "There are much worse places to spend one's life, I think."

She turned. "Ambition, desire, initiative . . ?"

He sighed. "I've had some unsettling thoughts of myself over the years, Kathleen. No sandals or ragged trousers or bare chest or beard, but at heart I suppose I could qualify in most other ways as a beachcomber. Ambition? Sorry about that."

They wandered round the gloomy house, inside and out, then stood a silent moment in the room where A. F. H. Friday had died. Here, the stillness was almost tangible. Even the air was stale from silence. She shuddered and led the way back outside, down off the veranda and along the well-worn path that took them back to the village.

They were half away along when she suddenly made a little sound and halted in mid-stride, pointing. Far out a pure white sail pitched beneath the pale enamel sky and a glossy hull rose out of the long troughs of sea to glide ahead then dip down to ride through another trough.

Alan said, "I'll be damned. Where'd he pop from?"

The sturdy little craft, broad-beamed and low-coupled, was lugger-built which meant she had no great speed under sail although on the other hand she could ride out some pretty rough seas, built as she was, never to capsize. But what puzzled Alan, and upon which he candidly remarked, she was coming from the wrong direction. She was approaching Emeraldia from due west. There was nothing in that direction for a great many miles. In fact there were no real docks in that direction until one hit mainland Hawaii, more than a thousand miles across the sun-warmed sea.

"Fishermen," she said, but he scotched that. For one thing the boat was far too clean, for another thing fishermen did not sail the South Pacific they motored it. Finally, as he pointed out, that vessel was clearly a pleasure craft.

"Well; surely people *do* sail this way, don't they? I mean, this time of year the ocean must have holidayers and yachtsmen sailing about."

That, he conceded, was possible. In fact, it was the only logical conclusion, for otherwise there wouldn't be any reason for people to come to Emeraldia.

They could see people beginning to congregate down by the wharf. Frank Chang and Ford Courtland were noticeable because they wore shirts while the natives did not. Even Mama Kameha was down there. Otherwise, there were about two dozen natives with more straggling along as word passed through the sleepy clearings where huts stood, that a strange ship was approaching.

Kathleen took Alan's hand and started hurrying along. "Come on; we can't be the only hold-outs. I'm as excited as everyone else is." She laughed at him, let go his hand and hastened on down the path.

CHAPTER EIGHT

Twins?

The vessel anchored a mile off shore. By that time everyone was murmuring in wonder. She carried a flag Ford Courtland swore was Panamanian. Frank went to look up the Panamanian flag in his encylopedia. When he returned he nodded at Alan's expression of enquiry. The flag was indeed Panamanian.

Mama Kameha, sweating fiercely in the hot sun, said he could sit out there with spyglasses and look the island over as long as he liked, she was going back into the shade of her restaurant-bar.

Courtland accepted the binoculars Frank offered him, made a slow study, and reported that a man dressed in white was on the bow with his own binoculars studying the people on the wharf.

Kathleen's exasperation made her say tartly that if the gentleman out there thought cannibals inhabited Emeraldia, the presence of the non-natives should convince him otherwise.

No one professed to understand why the stranger didn't sail on in and dock. The natives drifted away, all but a few with bumps of curiosity who went after their canoes to paddle out

76

and reconnoitre the newcomer.

Frank said it was the first time in his memory a boat had appeared and hadn't tied right up. He admitted to being puzzled but not exasperated, like Courtland was. Alan left Kathleen with Courtland and drifted back to the copra shed with Frank. "I suppose he's wearing out his C-Q call letters. The fact that we don't respond may make him a little chary, Frank."

Chang was indifferent. It was hot out and he'd stood in the sun until his shirt was dark with perspiration. "Back before the war Commissioner Friday had some pennants he used to run up a stripped tree behind Government House when ships came near. I don't know whatever became of those little flags. Anyway, that tree rotted and fell down. Hell, let him sit out there; when he needs fresh water, or gets his courage up, he'll be along."

Frank was right, but it wasn't until close to ten that night, which was well past the bedtime of everyone on Emeraldia, before the skipper of that functional sailing craft appeared, and then he didn't show up in the village but was taken by a native guide to Alan Barton's bungalow where his unexpected visit gave Alan a bad start out of a sound slumber.

The native laughed at Alan's surprise. He'd gone to the boat in his canoe, bolder than his friends, and had been hired to fetch the visitor ashore after dark. It didn't seem very odd to the native but as Alan stamped into boots and trousers it seemed damned odd to him.

Then he introduced himself out upon his veranda, shoved out a hand and turned to stone when the stranger introduced himself in turn.

"Ford Courtland, Mister Barton. Glad to know you."

Alan shook and withdrew his hand. "Ford Courtland," he repeated. "Is that what you said?"

"Yes. I'm Alfred Frederick Harold Friday's nephew."

Alan said, "That's very interesting. And you arrived today on that lugger beyond the bay?"

"Yes. I'd have come ashore earlier but you see we got caught out in something of a storm several days ago between Emeraldia and Roratonga and I've been at the pumps until today when we finally could get repairs under way."

"I see. The vessel is all right now, Mister Courtland?"

"Well, I have two crewmen aboard. They'll have everything shipshape in another day or two. We're well stocked with spares."

Alan dismissed the native, took his visitor inside, got a lamp lighted and went after his shirt. When he returned he studied the newcomer. "Do you have a wireless aboard?"

The newcomer said he had. His vessel was equipped with a very powerful set, in fact. He then asked why no one on the island replied when he'd called ashore. Alan explained and they smiled a little over the indifference which had allowed Commissioner Friday's old war-time wireless to fall into uselessness. Courtland thought it highly unusual for an island people to be content to be out of touch.

Alan said they had any number of radios on Emeraldia, and ever since he'd lived at Ibehlin, at any rate, there'd never been much actual reason to have wireless contact with the outside world.

"Emergencies?" asked Courtland, pursuing the topic with some vigour. "Illness? Perhaps a typhoon or a devastating fire, Mister Barton. And in the event of a poisoned appendix?"

Alan piqued, said, "You are unquestionably right, but you see, we manage here on Emeraldia. We didn't go hunting you — or other visitors to our island — they came hunting us." Then Alan removed some of the sting by smilingly concluding his reproof. "One of these days we'll repair the old set, of course." He offered his guest tea or coffee but the stranger had eaten shortly before coming ashore, so Alan got right down to what was bothering him.

"Would you mind telling me why you've come to Emeraldia, Mister Courtland?"

The stranger was lean and fit. He was a few years younger than his namesake blissfully slumbering in his cabin down at Mama Kameha's, and he acted much more poised, and yet he lacked the other man's physical power and his rough-tough assurance. When he answered Alan he sounded less and less like an Englishman, which Commissioner Friday's nephew was of course, but then as Alan reflected, the other chap didn't sound very English either.

"No, I don't mind, Mister Barton. I was in Honolulu when I heard of my uncle's death. When I finished up down there I decided to stop off on Emeraldia and see what progress has been made at bringing his murderer to justice."

Alan politely nodded. It was a good answer. In fact it seemed to be the stock answer for nephews of A. F. H. Friday. "Do you have any brothers?" asked Alan, "or perhaps cousins with a name similar to your's, Mister Courtland?"

The stranger shook his head and frowned softly as though he were beginning to have uneasy thoughts about Barton's rationale. "None."

Alan stood up. "I wonder if you'd go down to the village with me, Mister Courtland. There's a gentleman I'd like you to meet."

Courtland arose. "Bit late isn't it? Couldn't I come back in the morning?"

Alan was pleasant but he was also insistent. "This chap owns the warehouses you saw from the anchorage, Mister Courtland, he likes to personally welcome each newcomer arriving on Emeraldia. He would never forgive either of us if I didn't bring you along straightaway."

Courtland glanced at his watch, looked dubious, but he accompanied Alan out into the late night where shadows lay and where that handsome lugger shone off at her quiet anchorage, as two bright orange pinpricks of light in the otherwise empty and inky ocean.

As Alan took his visitor down to the northerly outskirts of town he kept up a pleasant little running conversation. The man with him seemed to lose some of his trepidation over paying someone a visit so late at night right up until Alan thumped Frank Chang's front door, then he said, in a voice full of protest, "Mister Barton; this will be the first place I've ever been where the people took pleasure from being aroused in the middle of the night. Hadn't we better . . . ?"

"On Emeraldia," said Alan drily, "we have some very unusual social customs." He banged on the door louder and when Frank appeared looking rumpled, puffy and annoyed, Alan said in the same dry tone, "Frank, this is Mister Ford Courtland. He came ashore about an hour ago from that lugger out in the harbour. Mister Courtland, this is Frank Chang who was a very close friend of your uncle."

They shook hands with Frank looking just as bewildered over the identity of his guest as Alan had been. He stepped aside, motioned for them both to enter, and when Courtland began protesting all over again, Frank, clutching a robe to his frame, came wide awake as he assured the newcomer he was delighted to be awakened under the circumstances. He then got a light going, went to slip into some clothing and when he returned he said, "Ford Courtland?" When the yachtsman nodded he then said, "You'll have clearance papers with your name on them, won't you, Mister Courtland, and perhaps a wireless permit?"

Courtland looked at Frank as though he were round the bend. Instead of answering he fished inside a pocket and tossed a letter upon Frank's parlour table. "My name is on this," he said a trifle stiffly. "It's the letter you sent along with my uncle's effects, Mister Chang. As for other identification — I have licences aboard the *Eleuthera.*"

Frank stood staring at the letter. He raised his eyes to Alan. Barton merely shrugged and took a chair. Courtland, who seemed to be a testy individual, studied them both then said, "Are you always so suspicious of visitors, Mister Chang?"

Frank picked up the letter and examined it as he replied. "Not always, Mister Courtland. Only when they bring little mysteries with them." He was satisfied the letter was genuine and handed it back. "Do you have a brother?"

"No, I have no brother, and Mister Barton has already asked me that."

"All right, Mister Courtland. Then can you explain to us who would be using the same name?"

Courtland blinked. "My name?"

Frank nodded. "About a month ago another Ford Courtland dropped in on us. Large, husky chap, about your age or maybe a bit younger."

Courtland remained silent for a bit. He looked enquiringly at Alan. Barton nodded his head in corroboration of Frank's allegation. "Is this man still on Emeraldia?"

Frank answered quietly. "He's probably blissfully sleeping right this minute in a cabin in the centre of town."

Courtland went to a chair, sat down, leaned on the table and looked a little blank as he digested what seemed to be a total surprise to him. Finally he said, "But; why?"

Alan spoke up. "That doesn't interest me as much right now as knowing which of you men is the real Ford Courtland."

That was something the newcomer seemed able to handle. He arose, turning brisk. "If you have a boat we can go out to the *Eleuthera*, gentlemen, and I can show you plenty of official evidence of my identity."

Frank at once arose. "I just happen to have a canoe under the dock. Come along, Alan, we couldn't pick a better time, while everyone is asleep."

They were all standing now. Courtland delayed them a bit by saying, "I don't understand what his purpose would be; not here on Emeraldia at any rate. If he forged cheques or something like that it would make some sense."

"He has money, Mister Courtland. He hasn't done anything that would be a discredit to your name — or someone's name. He's quite pleasant."

"What reason does he give for being here?"

"I rather imagine it's the same reason you'll give. He is interested in why Commissioner Friday was killed."

Courtland muttered a swear word. "This seems very weird, gentlemen. And suppose, in the morning when we confront this man, he turns out to be — well — violent?"

Frank smiled. "By morning we'll be prepared for that. Shall we go now?"

"Yes, of course."

Frank led off. Alan managed to stay beside Ford Courtland in an effort that was rather obvious; he had no intention of giving the stranger a chance to do anything troublesome. Courtland saw how this was and looked less resentful than exasperated.

Frank Chang's canoe had no motor so they had to paddle, which took some time since the lugger had anchored beyond the immediate confines of the harbour. Alan muttered something about this and Courtland said his charts of the area were sketchy; he had feared running foul of shoals.

When they reached the lugger the moon was far down the sky and there was a faint pink blush of pre-dawn light over against the dusty sky where the ocean lay as smooth as dull glass.

This was the coldest time of day — or night — and it was still amply warm to make the paddlers and their passenger feel comfortable.

Courtland led the way aboard. If either of his crewmen were on watch neither Barton nor Chang saw them as they ducked low to enter the wide, handsome cabin below decks where a lamp was quickly lit and their host went at once to a metal locker bolted to a wall and began pulling out old clearance papers, licences, quarantine stickers, even a number of letters addressed to him and postmarked 'Honolulu, Hawaii' dating back many months.

As far as Alan and Frank could determine, they were in the presence of the real Ford Courtland, and if that should have been very reassuring, it wasn't for the basic reason that they now had another mystery on their hands; Who was the *other* Ford Courtland, the one back on Emeraldia?

CHAPTER NINE

A Little Strategy

Courtland satisfied Barton and Chang not only who he actually was, but by means of that powerful wireless aboard his *Eleuthera* he contacted three freighters in the Caribbean, also sailing under the Panamanian Registry, which belonged to him. He was a moderately successful Western Hemisphere shipping magnate and although, as he explained, he'd been born and reared in Britain, after the war he'd gone to sea on commercial vessels, ending up a number of years later with his own shipping business.

The residence in London where Frank had sent the Commissioner's private effects was still owned and resided in by Mister Courtland's maiden sister. It had been she who'd ultimately got the news to Courtland in Honolulu about the Commissioner's death.

None of it sounded very far-fetched to Frank and Alan as they shared a mug of coffee with their host aboard the *Eleuthera,* but, as Frank pointed out, the more prosaic one story sounded, the more impossible the other one appeared.

Courtland kept hammering away at one thing: "What the devil is his game? As I understand it my uncle was not a wealthy man when he was killed. Then why would anyone bother going to all this trouble, and risk, to impersonate his nephew?"

The only thing Frank could come up with was the obvious answer. "It is worthwhile. Whatever is behind it is very worthwhile, otherwise no one would be doing it. There's another point too — how do we explain about you, Mister Courtland? You can't come ashore using the name Ford Courtland. Your crewmen can't go ashore either, unless we can come up with a believable lie."

Alan Barton went to a porthole and stood gazing shoreward. "Can you contact the Jenkins newspaper syndicate headquarters in London," he asked without looking around, "and ascertain whether or not they have a lady reporter in their employ named Kathleen Scott, presently on assignment to Emeraldia Island?"

Courtland said he could do that very easily, and providing the Jenkins people co-operated, he should have an answer back within three or four hours. He then said, addressing Frank, "Suppose we do something like that with our Mister Imposter Courtland?"

Frank was agreeable except for one thing. They knew nothing about the impersonator beyond his feigned background.

"And the fact that he chartered an aircraft to drop him on the island," said Alan from the window. "Start the tracing at the charter service where he hired the airplane and go from there."

Frank and Ford Courtland nodded almost in unison. Courtland, looking at Alan's back, said, "You were right about the advantages of having that wireless out of commission, Mister Barton. Only the three of us will know what we're about."

Alan turned, yawning behind a hand. "Frank, we'd better paddle back. People will be able to see the canoe shortly now, and that could raise some curiosity we'd have to explain away with some fancy lying." As Chang arose Alan went back towards the gangway leading out of the below-decks cabin and smiled at their host. "If you're not all you seem to be, Mister Courtland, I'm going to throw in the sponge and migrate to some other island. I never cared for mysteries."

Courtland's eyes glinted with hard humour. "Don't pack anything just yet, Mister Barton. I'll manage to convince you yet. Now then — do I come ashore this afternoon?"

Frank said, "Yes. Using another name and calling yourself a pearl dealer, artifacts collector, anything you like. Look me up around my copra sheds. You'll want to meet the other Ford Courtland. And bring the answers to those wireless enquiries too, if they've come back to you by then."

Barton and Chang slid down the side of the *Eleuthera* to Frank's canoe, waved at Courtland who was on the deck watching, then pushed off and started paddling. There wasn't a chance of them reaching the Ibehlin dock before full sunrise, which was when the islanders were beginning to stir, so they struck out towards the nearest shoreline in order to follow that around as though they might have been fishing. Since there were no fishing poles in the canoe any close observer could have seen the fallacy to this illusion, but as Frank said, "You can't win them all."

He also said, "What made you throw in that bit about Kathleen Scott; don't you believe she's genuine either?"

Alan didn't specify whether he considered her genuine or not, he simply said, "He's got the wireless, Frank, and it will clear things up a bit if he uses it to prove anything at all. As far as Kathleen is concerned — I don't know. Since this other Courtland barged in on me in my sleep last night I'm not sure what I ought to believe."

For a while they paddled in silence. They got over next to a dark length of shore which camouflaged them quite well, upped-oars to let the tide carry them for a bit and Alan had a cigarette for breakfast. The sun was rising beyond the island. All the harbour, the promontory, even the sea southward and beyond, was golden lighted, but the lee-side of the island where the village and the shallows lay, was still in semi-shadow. By the time Frank and Alan took up the oars and paddled towards the beach near Frank's sheds, the sun was just beginning to edge over the spiny, lush low ridge which formed the spine of Emeraldia, but by then they were within a few yards of home.

Not that it mattered all that much, their having been out to the lugger. It would only eliminate the need for complicated prevarications. The way both men felt as they tiredly trudged to Frank's bungalow for breakfast, there were already enough complications.

They had coffee, fried eggs, tasty but rubbery octopus with their eggs, and during the course of the meal someone in the shed coaxed the conveyor-belt engine to life. Frank looked up.

"Another dull, routine day in the life of the castaways of Emeraldia," he said, and laughed. "I wish the people who've told me I had to be a little balmy to want to live like this in a world of utter boredom could drop in right now."

Alan wasn't receptive. "No thanks. Let's get rid of all the current crop of visitors before any more come along. Frank . . . ? There's something in the back of my skull."

"According to all the medical books I've got there is supposed to be."

"Did Ford Courtland — the first one — ask you a lot of questions about the Commissioner and the wartime Japanese?"

"He asked."

"Yesterday Kathleen Scott did the same to me. The reason it stuck in my head was the

90

look on her face and something she said; something about it not being difficult to go to Tokyo and dig up the names of the Japs who commanded here during the war."

Frank finished eating, squinted at his watch then said, "Why would that stick in your mind?"

"Because it was important to her who those Japs were."

Frank started to rise, then settled back and reached for the coffee pot, filled both their cups and frowned while he wrestled with some thought that seemed to annoy more than interest him. Eventually he said, "Alan, I'll confess to also having a thought. It occurred to me last week that while Courtland — the one on the island — was cultivating me, the woman was avoiding me and making a point of cultivating you. Now, simply because I'm a devious Chinese by nature, it struck me that those two, who are very close and chummy otherwise, ask me questions, ask you questions, then compare the answers over drinks later on."

Alan, to whom the idea of collusion was quite new, didn't touch his coffee but he did light a smoke as he considered Frank's suggestion. Eventually he said, "And if they *do* know one another and *did* come here at different times faking their identities, it's got to have something to do with the wartime Japanese." At Frank's sceptical expression Alan made a hand-gesture. "What else, for Pete's sake?"

91

"What is the point, you should ask," stated Frank. "The Japs were here and they departed. Emeraldia was nothing but a back-bay for their evacuation hospital units. Nothing very glorious nor even very admirable about that. Moreover, they weren't here more than eighteen months."

"Do you recall the three who returned a couple of years ago; the ones Commissioner Friday played host to?"

"I distinctly remember, because I'm always uneasy around Japanese. What about them?"

"Frank, did they really only come here to groan a little over their little cemetery, or was it something else?"

"For instance . . ?"

"How in hell would I know," exploded Alan. "You were Commissioner Friday's confidant. All he ever said to me was that they'd come and he felt sorry for them. What did he tell *you* about their visit?"

"The same. He didn't like the Japanese. No one did who was around the South Pacific in those days — excepting of course the other Japanese — but after a few days he felt sorry for those chaps. Especially the one whose son was buried here."

Alan jumped up and strode to the door and back. "There's more, Frank. There's got to be. Not only more, but Commissioner Friday knew what it was, and now this fake Ford Courtland and this Kathleen Scott, if that's her name,

92

they've got to know whatever it is."

Frank began clearing the table. When he'd finished he said, "All right. Give me an hour to see that everything is going properly in the sheds, then I'll drive up to your bungalow, pick you up, and we'll go nosing around a little."

"Nosing around?"

"Some of the people over on the back of the island were helpers at that old Jap installation during the war. I know from listening to my workers speak of it that *our* Ford Courtland and Miss Scott have spent days over there asking questions. Belatedly, you and I might start doing the same thing."

Alan was agreeable, but he reminded Chang they'd have to be back at Ibehlin before mid-afternoon when the *Eleuthera*'s master would come to see them. He then went on up through the trees to his residence, shaved, bathed, put on fresh clothing and glanced out the open door just in time to see Kathleen Scott tramping up the path towards his front porch. He went out to meet her and found that she wanted him to get Commissioner Friday's old files for her.

She had a plausible excuse for wishing to see them. "He was such a colourful individual, Alan. After we got back to town last night and I had time to reflect, it occurred to me that he'd make a very good book just by himself. I've even thought of a title for it: *Commissioner Of Paradise*."

He smiled and offered her a chair without

93

making any comment on that title, although he certainly had a private thought or two respecting it. He said Frank Chang had all the old files. He also said, "You don't need me to get them for you; just go ask Frank, he'll let you see them."

She bridled over that. "Well, of course I could do that, Alan, but I don't know Frank all that well and it seemed to me that he might misconstrue my purpose. While with you — well — you'd understand. Aside from being a fellow-writer you're more gentle, Alan, more understanding."

He returned her tender smile and said of course he'd get the old files. That in fact if she'd like, he'd prepare a native supper for two this very night and they could go over the files together here at this bungalow.

She acquiesced so readily he wondered afterwards as he watched her depart back down the path towards the village whether, if he hadn't made the suggestion, she might not have made it herself.

Alan sighed. It was hard, being a lonely man with naughty suspicions about a beautiful woman. If he could have been perhaps ten years younger he wouldn't be so disgustingly suspicious, and then of course he'd be able to keep his mind on other things tonight by candlelight when they were alone with the soft sound of the surf to soothe them into a romantic mood.

By the time Frank arrived in the Land-Rover, Alan was pitying himself. He was also angry with himself. He piled into the Rover blurting out the story of Kathleen's visit and looking morose. Frank smiled without commenting upon the more promising aspect of the forthcoming supper, and agreed to hand over the files. He said he'd been over them so many times he knew them by heart, and if there was any clue in them about what this entire affair was about, he'd be unreservedly astonished.

They then took the bouncy ruts leading through the island's humid and greeny jungle towards the far side of the island where that old Japanese facility had been, snug against the base of the island's only hog-back spine of a hill.

CHAPTER TEN

A Total Surprise

Frank parked his Land-Rover in the centre of a low, flat spot that once had held a number of camouflaged tents. It was still possible after a quarter of a century to see that some kind of orderly cantonment had stood in this spot.

Frank, who had no recollection at all of what had once stood here, nonetheless had heard enough stories to be fairly explicit. But as he said, when and if they wished for an accurate description, they'd continue on to the villages beyond the hill which lay along the island's far curving shoreline, and bring one of the older people back who would remember this place well.

"But I have no idea what good that would do," he concluded. "Here we are, there are the little squares of stones the Japs used around the base of their tents, and just what in the hell good is all this doing us?"

Alan laughed. "We'd better just get on over to the villages and start asking questions. This place doesn't offer much of a message."

They went to where the small Japanese cemetery lay, mostly overgrown now but evidently, only a short while back, perhaps a matter of

96

two or three years, brushed out clean. The lianas were reaching for sucker-trees and a staggering variety of ground-cover was beginning to form an interlocking carpet again.

It was the ominous, tell-tale mounds that made it so obvious what this place was.

There were sawn stumps showing where the original planners of this spot had cut away trees, bushes, had even manhandled great lichen-speckled boulders to create an acre of peaceful serenity in the heart of a jungle. Rocks formed an uneven low wall. There had once been some kind of teak altar.

"Shinto," said Frank Chang, giving his shoulders a little toss. "Must have been a discouraging sight for the old boys who came back after twenty years or more, to see how the jungle was going to eventually swallow everything. Still, they'd been through jungle countries before. If the one whose son is here wished, I suppose he could have the remains taken back to Japan."

Alan pointed. "What about that altar? Wasn't there more to it?"

"There was more, but maybe the natives took it."

"What for; are they Shintoists too?"

Frank smiled. "They're nothing. Or maybe I should have said they are spirit worshippers if they are anything. The fact is, as you know by now, they aren't religious at all. They have a sort of belief about spirits living in the air, in the trees, in the sea, in the rocks, but why should anyone already living in paradise need God? They get just enough rain — they never have to pray for more. The sun shines three hundred and sixty days out of the year — they don't have to believe in a Sun-God. Food is everywhere." Frank smiled. "Not much point in relying on the supernatural when you don't need Him, is there?"

Where the little altar had once stood there was little left now excepting four poles planted in the ground, and where had once been a frond-roof, rotten old sagging poles hung. Stone masonry had formed the base of the altar but whatever had rested upon the topmost stone was gone. Frank agreed that a native had undoubtedly taken it, but as a foundation stone for a hut, an anchor for a canoe, or perhaps as the base for a stone oven, not as anything of religious significance.

Alan went among the graves, found several with rusted metal nameplates upon which Japanese symbols had been painted in white, and correctly assumed these plates went with field-hospitals to be used as grave-markers, and upon whose surface were painted the dead soldier's name, number, and date of death. The plates were nearly rusted away, the names were no longer legible except in one or two cases, and it didn't matter anyway, as Frank Chang said, who was under each mound, because he was going nowhere; would not need a rank or serial number or name again.

There was one grave, no different from the others except that it had a bronze nameplate which was a thick and weighty casting. Frank said, "That's the administrative officer's son. I saw this nameplate before they brought it over here. Mister Friday showed it to me. It cost the old boy a lot of money; this kind of thing is very expensive in Japan. But it'll endure — if that's important — so the old man and his family can make their pilgrimages here from time to time and find the grave."

They stood looking at the plaque. It was clearly a work of art, for although it was quite unadorned, each Japanese symbol was meticulously formed and shaped, and where the name in English stood forth — Akira Yamamoto — great detail had been spent getting each letter precisely as it should be. Alan said the name in English probably indicated the Japanese suspicion that Emeraldia would remain in the hands of English-speaking people and never become Japanese property.

Frank shrugged that off. "If they didn't need Emeraldia when they were island-hopping towards Mainland U.S. during the war, what would they want it for now? Come along; let's get on over to the villages and see if we can find out what Miss Scott and her fake friend, Courtland, have been trying to get out of the natives."

They didn't even get back to the Land-Rover.

They went from the cemetery back to the flat area where the old Japanese evacuation hospital had been, paused a moment to look around, then started on. Two natives who had evidently been watching for some time, moved forth into the clearing and smiled into the startled faces of Barton and Chang. Both natives wore wristwatches, the badge on Emeraldia that a person had been off the island to work, perhaps to either New Zealand or Australia, although they occasionally went as far as Hawaii — the difficulty here of course was that they rarely ever returned from Hawaii — and sometimes, as seamen, they visited Indonesia or perhaps Japan, the Philippines, or sometimes even Malaysia. All those wristwatches really guaranteed was that these two stalwart, grinning natives had seen something of the world beyond Emeraldia. Frank knew them. They had worked for him the year previous, but had given up steady employment to move back to the villages over on the far side of the island where loafing was an art instead of a minor sin, as it was around Chang's sheds, dock and warehouses, at Ibehlin.

Frank asked what the natives were doing. They said they'd left their villages the day before heading for Ibehlin, had been walking ever since, and had spent the night not far from the old Japanese hospital site. They then asked the same question of Frank. He was candid. "Trying to figure out what's so important about this place that people still come from off the island to visit it."

One of the dusky men pointed. "Grave over there with an iron plate on it."

Frank nodded. "One Jap soldier. He wasn't even an officer — at least not a very high one. I don't see why anyone except maybe his father and mother should care about him."

"They do," said the grinning big native. "Two of them were in the villages about the same time that man and woman from Ibehlin were over there also asking questions."

Frank and Alan looked blankly at the natives. Alan said, "Two *Japanese?*"

"Yeah. They wanted to know who among us had been around when that hospital was here. They wrote down the names of some of the older people." The native who was speaking chuckled as though drolly amused. "They went away in a motor-boat but they didn't fool anyone."

"They didn't?" breathed Alan.

"No. The people found tracks where another pair of them went scouting all around between the beaches and this place, while their friends were asking questions."

Alan dug for his cigarette packet, offered it around then held a match for everyone to light up. The natives only smoked because the non-natives were known to do it. More often than not their only pleasure from the ordeal was co-piously watering eyes and a condition of near apoplexy to keep from coughing, unless, as with these two, they'd been away from Emeraldia, then they sometimes were habitual smokers. However, these two were not, they puffed and grinned and puffed, but they were careful to spit out the smoke as soon as it got into their mouths.

"Four Japanese," said Frank, enunciating clearly so there'd be no chance of any misunderstanding. "Four Japanese came to Emeraldia — when — last week?"

"Last week, yeah."

"And asked about this old Japanese graveyard and hospital place?"

"Yeah. Two asked among the villages. The other two went slipping all around thinking no one would see, or know they were here."

Frank looked at Alan then said to the natives: "Why?"

Neither Emeraldian knew. "Same like the man who dropped here out of the airplane, and the woman: To ask a lot of questions. Why they ask, I don't know."

"What kind of questions?"

"Not about the best fishing places. Oh; about this place. And over there where the graves are. And Commissioner Friday. And about you two, and Mama Kameha, and those two strangers. Just a lot of talk." The big native smiled very broadly. "They had plenty of *sake,* plenty of time, we had plenty of fish to fry, so everyone talked a lot."

"I see. Then they went away?"

"Yeah. But the other two must have already gone away because we never seen them. We all went down to the beach to see the pair that visited us paddle away, but that other pair — we never seen them go, only the tracks and marks and where they'd stopped to camp and sleep and eat."

Frank looked at Alan and said, "Nice. Very nice. How do you like this?"

Alan was honest. "Not much."

One of the natives, grinning like an idol, said, "You going back to Ibehlin pretty soon: we'll ride along."

Frank said they'd be going back but not very soon; he'd take the men if they wanted to wait a bit. They withdrew to the jungle-fringe to sit and relax and wait. They were in no hurry, had never been in a hurry in their lives.

Frank and Alan slow-paced their way around the old hospital site until Frank stopped them both with a question. "I'm beginning to get a little scared, how about you?"

Alan halted. "Try this, Frank: No native killed the Commissioner. Neither you nor I did it. So that leaves outsiders. It would be very simple for people to come here, pitch a concealed camp along one of the far-side beaches and not be discovered by the natives if they really wanted to work at *not* being discovered."

"Japanese," said Frank.

Alan didn't bother to specify who his hypothetical people were. It wasn't necessary anyway since all they'd been thinking about for an hour and more now had been Japanese.

"One of them slips over to Government House and shoots the Commissioner."

"Why?"

"I don't know."

"All right. After they shoot him they all pack up and sail away." Frank gently wagged his head. "Why again? They didn't rob him. I knew every drawer in that place, Alan. I've told you this before. Nothing was touched. Nothing at all. So just give me some idea why a little band of Japs would sneak to Emeraldia just to kill the only person here who earned their endless gratitude by reclaiming the graves for them, then slip away again without taking anything."

Alan raised his hands in exasperation. "I can't come up with anything, Frank. I'm only trying to feel my way as far as the thing goes."

Frank nodded. "Yeah, and as far as it goes it keeps getting murkier and murkier. But at least we've finally got a suspect — a band of suspects — to Mister Friday's murder, and for the first time I'm beginning to feel something other than philosophical about that killing." Frank turned towards his Land-Rover smiling. "I'm beginning to feel like a man who wants some revenge for the death of a friend."

"You don't like Japs, Frank."

"That's true. Come on, let's get back to the village; Courtland ought to be coming ashore

104

within the next hour or so." Frank raised an arm to make a beckoning gesture to the pair of grinning natives. They rose at once from their shady places and came over to climb into the Land-Rover. It was a memorable delight to ride in Frank's car. There were only two cars on Emeraldia and one of those — a vintage Austin — was gently rusting away in a shed in the village where Commissioner Friday, its owner, had parked it many years before when he'd been unable to get replacement parts for it. That made Frank Chang's Land-Rover the only vehicle, therefore a ride in it was something to be remembered with pleasure.

Frank's vehicle had definite limitations; for one thing the island only had one full-length road. For another, getting Captain Voermann to bring in barrels of auto fuel was extremely costly. And finally, almost everywhere Frank went in the course of a day's work could be reached more quickly on foot. Still, the Land-Rover was a prestigious possession, even when all it did was sit and swelter in the shade.

CHAPTER ELEVEN

Alan Barton's Suggestion

It was inevitable that when Ford Courtland put off from his anchored lugger people should notice and pass the word around. After all, as far as most islanders knew, no one had come ashore from the strange vessel since it had dropped anchor the day before.

Frank and Alan heard from the copra workers out in the curing area that a motor-launch was coming. It was by then two in the afternoon. They went down to the dock where a few loafers were beginning to congregate, among them the imposter named Courtland, and Kathleen Scott. This time Mama Kameha came padding on worn sandals exactly as she was, not bothering to adorn her heavy mane with the broad ribbon she usually wore when visitors arrived. She told Frank a couple of beer-guzzling natives had told her earlier in the day there was a rumour going round among the village people that someone had come ashore from the lugger in the night. She wrinkled her face sceptically.

"You know when they don't have anything to talk about they make something up."

Frank agreed smoothly and drifted over

where the fake Courtland was standing, shading his eyes. A few yards distant Alan was with Kathleen Scott. Frank could imagine how Kathleen was viewing the arrival of another visitor to the island.

The burly, powerful man at Frank's side said, "Do you ever get health inspectors or quarantine officials — people like that, Frank?"

The answer was as Frank gave it. "Not any more. When I was a kid we'd get some kind of official once or twice a year, but only if Commissioner Friday wirelessed for one. Usually when there was an epidemic of malaria or fish-poisoning. If you think that's what this chap could be, I doubt it very much. Even in the old days they didn't come unless called for. Now, we don't have a working wireless."

When the motor-launch began its curve to approach the dock broadsides several grinning natives moved to catch the rope which would be thrown to them. By then Frank recognised the lean, leather-dark man in the boat, but despite his misgivings, Courtland carried it off very well.

He passed both the natives who'd helped him tie up a silver coin. Frank heard the imposter grunt, "American," under his breath. Frank had also seen the silver coins, had recognised them as being of U.S. issue. Then the real Ford Courtland and the imitation one faced one another as the real one suavely said, "Charles Dawes, gentlemen, dealer in marine supplies out of Honolulu."

Everyone shook hands. When Frank's eyes crossed the direct glance of 'Mister Dawes' not a flicker of recognition was visible. The imposter said, "Out of Honolulu, Mister Dawes? How come the Panamanian flag?"

Dawes smiled apologetically while Frank held his breath. "Tax-dodge, Mister Courtland. Of course I prefer not to pay any more taxes than you do; under U.S. Registry I'd have to pay tax on everything I haul, sell or trade, not to mention health and compensation tax on crewmen, tax on an export-import licence — the lot. Under Panamanian Registry I'm practically taxfree."

'Mister Dawes' made a slight and gallant little bow towards Kathleen Scott. "I'd heard the natives out here were very handsome people, but I wasn't prepared for you, my dear."

Kathleen smiled, Frank and Alan smiled, and Mama Kameha rolled up her eyes as though to say nothing ever changed in this department. Ford Courtland studied 'Mister Dawes' from eyes that seemed to Frank to be steadily losing their suspicion. 'Mister Dawes' next move just about clinched it, and Frank had to admit to himself that the real Ford Courtland was an excellent actor. He said, "I heard there was no wireless on Emeraldia. Now that's a mighty poor condition to permit to exist. Suppose there was a major disaster?"

Alan said, "We have a wireless. It just doesn't work. Hasn't worked for several years."

'Mister Dawes' smiled. "I have a locker of parts aboard the *Eleuthera*. Reasonably priced too." He continued to smile. "But we can do business later." He glanced across the broad roadway where Mama Kameha's place stood. "I'll stand a round, folks. The first round is on Charlie Dawes."

It went like that for a solid hour. In fact by the time Frank could pry 'Mister Dawes' away he and his impersonator, 'Ford Courtland', had become quite friendly. They seemed to have been in a good many places in the South Pacific, seemed to know a number of people each other knew.

Frank offered to show 'Mister Dawes' the old wireless. Alan Barton had left the building a half hour earlier, but when Courtland and Frank Chang finally appeared, Alan was dozing in the shade outside Frank's bungalow. He gave them both a critical glance, obviously annoyed by their dalliance at Mama Kameha's bar, but all he said was, "Good job of selling, Mister Courtland."

Inside the bungalow they each took a chair in Frank's shadowy parlour where the heat was just beginning to filter in, and Courtland wordlessly produced several slips of paper, leaned to place them upon a low, teakwood coffee table without offering them to either Frank or Alan, and said, "The plot thickens, lads. There's the reply from Jenkins Syndicate on Miss Scott — no such person in their employ, never has been — and there is a report from the charter service that dropped Mister Courtland on your beach month before last, giving me the numbers they copied off his Maritime Union card, auto operator's licence, and whatnot. Those other two papers are from the San Francisco office of the Maritime Union, and from a friend of mine who dug into the U.S. Social Security files to come up with a name for the man whose Social Security number was listed on the Maritime Union reports for one Herbert Dentzel, former pilot, ship's officer, aircraft and boat dealer, most recently engaged in the importation business handling primarily Japanese *objets d'art*."

Ford Courtland leaned back looking satisfied with himself, and of course he had held the undivided attention of his audience throughout the entire recitation. But now Alan said, "No criminal record?" and Courtland shook his head. "I kept digging for that, too," he said, looking disappointed. "Of course impersonation isn't legal."

Frank brushed that aside. "It wouldn't be any more than a misdemeanour. But he hasn't used your name for any worthwhile purpose yet."

"Hasn't he then? Can you say without equivocation, Mister Chang, that this impersonator didn't kill my uncle; can you prove he's not a murderer?"

110

Frank looked at Alan then said, "*Prove* it? Well; I'd have a hell of a time proving it, of course, but how about those records you dug up on the man — was he anywhere close to Emeraldia at the date of the murder?"

Courtland didn't reply to that but he dropped his gaze to the papers on the coffee-table as though at least Frank's idea had merit in his view. Then he said, "Give me one valid reason why he impersonated me?"

Alan sounded slightly impatient when he spoke up next. "He knew Commissioner Friday had a nephew. A little research would prove this nephew wasn't known on Emeraldia. Why? Well; because this man knows something your uncle also knew — and this man probably guessed someone else here might help him get some answers if they thought he was the Commissioner's kinsman."

Courtland opened his mouth to speak but Alan held up a hand. "I'm not through. You asked how we knew this man didn't kill your uncle. We don't *know* it, but personally I believe a Japanese killed him."

Courtland scowled. "A Japanese. Are there some on Emeraldia?"

Frank said drily, "Not now, apparently, but there evidently were when your uncle was shot to death." Frank launched into an explanation and Courtland sat like stone taking it all in. When Frank finished the story as related to him by the two natives that very morning over against the jungly spine that separated one side of Emeraldia from the other side, Courtland threw himself back in his chair, pushed out long legs and gazed from Frank to Alan with an expression of genuine dismay.

"Are you gentlemen implying that my old uncle had made some astonishing discovery concerning the Japanese who were here on Emeraldia a quarter century ago, and he was murdered to silence him?"

Alan lit a cigarette which conveniently kept him from having to reply. Frank ran a hand through his hair, looked out a window where the copra lay baking in hot sunlight, and did not answer either.

"What discovery?" demanded Ford Courtland in a loud voice. "There was one of those forlorn little field hospitals on this island for not even two years before the Japanese surrendered. There was nothing as trivial in the entire Pacific War as such a place."

Frank explained about the bronze plaque on the Japanese grave, about the Japanese who had returned to visit Emeraldia during Commissioner Friday's lifetime. But if there was a connection between that visit, the grave, and the death of Courtland's uncle, Frank made no attempt to point it out. He simply said, "It is in my opinion some secret relating to that camp, the graveyard, or the officers who commanded here. Prove it? Hell; I can't even prove there were four Japanese sneaking around here only last week, Mister Courtland."

Courtland sat in dour thought for a moment then came up with a logical — but pointless — idea. "There are bound to be natives here who remember those Japanese. We can . . ."

"Forget it," muttered Alan Barton. "They don't know."

"How can you be sure of that?"

"Because, if they *did* know, by now the man who is impersonating you and his wife — or whatever she is — would be gone. They've been going out every damned day for nearly two months pumping everyone in sight. She's got me down for a session over candlelight and *sake* this very evening, and no one has told them the right answers yet. No one. They don't know any more today than when they landed here two months back, Mister Courtland."

The lean, hawkish newcomer shook his head at them. "No one knows, perhaps. My uncle may have died being the only one."

"Try again," said Frank Chang somewhat caustically.

"Those Japs knew *something:* Otherwise they wouldn't have come here. Wouldn't have killed your uncle. Wouldn't have returned again after killing your uncle."

Courtland got to his feet, pocketed both hands and stalked to the window to gaze out where shimmering sunlight worked very efficiently at dehydrating all those hundreds upon hundreds of coconut halves. He wrinkled his nose and turned back to sombrely regard his companions.

"Some secret record that may have been left here? What in the hell could be of any great importance this long after the war; even some unknown treaty, astonishing in nature, wouldn't cause much of a ripple now, when people are worrying about the next one, not the last one."

Alan put out his cigarette and went to get a drink of water in Frank's immaculate little kitchen. He called to ask if the others would care for a drink. They wouldn't so he drank alone and returned to the chair he'd vacated.

He said, "Treasure."

Frank's black eyes came round slowly. Ford Courtland's brows dropped lower above his slatey eyes. The room was silent for as long as Alan let it remain that way.

"It has bothered me ever since the Commissioner was killed. Not *who* did it, but *why* it was done. Okay; I'll let you in on my research about something that actually is no great secret but which is nonetheless very little publicised even now, so many years later.

"The Japanese had two highly specialized teams of plunderers — that's my word, not their word — who went ashore with every assault outfit that hit the beaches of Pacific islands. One team went immediately for the local treasury. The other team struck immediately at local banks, if there were any, and if not then they struck at whatever trader's establishment

114

that had the biggest steel safe. They had some heavy expenses, financing their Pacific War. These teams helped defray the cost. They took one million in gold and silver from Castle Island, a hundred miles east of here. They got something like thirty-one million from Singapore. From Guam, some of the other U.S. islands, they got a lot less, but in total it was a hell of a lot of loot. Millions. Not always in gold and silver, but negotiable.

"They were still doing this shortly before the war ended, but by then it was hazardous as hell trying to slip the loot back to Japan by sea or air."

"Here?" breathed Ford Courtland. "Here, on Emeraldia — buried here?"

Alan said he had no idea, no proof at all that anything was buried on Emeraldia. "No one knows how much was actually taken; no one is even sure how much restitution was ever made. But I'll tell you one thing, chaps; there is a staggering discrepancy in the most reliable of official figures. There *could* be — mind now, I'm not saying there is — but there damned well could be upwards of twenty millions in paper, gold and silver, hidden on Emeraldia, because at least that much never reached Japan at all, and it is somewhere in the South Pacific, according to all the authorities!"

CHAPTER TWELVE

Plain Talk — and Moonlight

Improbable though Alan's suggestion seemed at the moment, nonetheless, as he pointed out, there was an enormous amount of money *somewhere* in the South Pacific, and while it may not have ever touched Emeraldia, one thing was palpably certain — it was *somewhere* outside of Japan.

Frank finally said, "I suppose it would be hard to imagine a more plausible reason for murder than twenty millions of dollars."

Ford Courtland grunted. "Twenty thousand — *two* thousand — would be considered more than ample reason in most places I've been, gentlemen." He bent a long, long stare upon Alan. "It's frightfully fantastic. You'll pardon me for saying that I hope."

Alan, in the act of glancing at his wrist, raised his head and smiled. "I'll pardon you for anything you want to think, Mister Courtland. I'll only argue one issue with you — a murder was committed, I saw the corpse myself. There was a reason for that killing. Beyond that you can conjecture to hell and back; more power to you. This is the total of everything I could arrive with. I won't even feel very pleased if I'm correct, because it stands out in my mind that if those assassins know where the stuff is cached, and if they killed the Commissioner because he also knew, then they just might get some looney idea you or Frank or I also know — and that could be damned painful."

"But Mister Friday *didn't* know," put in Frank. "One of those Japs stuck a gun in his chest and told him to spit it out or he'd die. He couldn't tell them so they kept their word."

Alan shrugged. "I thought of that too, Frank. I also got another thought; suppose he *did* know and told them, *then* they shot him to keep him silent?"

"No good," muttered Courtland. "It doesn't hold water, Mister Barton, because if he'd known, and if he'd told them, they wouldn't still be poking about asking questions, they'd have dug up the stuff and cleared out long ago."

Frank, sunk in thought, roused himself and said, "How did that Herbert Dentzel character find out? How did the woman named Scott find out? How come so many people know answers to something Alan and I, who were friends of your uncle and visited with him every single day, had no inkling of?"

Courtland had no answer but he had a tough suggestion. "Suppose, Mister Barton, when you keep that engagement tonight that you mentioned, with Miss Scott, that Mister Chang and I drop in and elicit a few answers."

Alan looked steadily at the tall, lean man. "Just what do you mean when you use the term — elicit?"

Courtland smiled thinly and said nothing. Alan shook his head. "No thanks. I'll try and get something without twisting any arms."

"All right," concurred Courtland. "Then perhaps if I brought my two crewmen ashore we could catch Mister Dentzel and get him to give us some answers."

Alan began a slow scowl but Frank spoke out before the conversation could get rough-edged. "Forget these two. They are harmless. It's those Japanese I'm worried about. You can bet your money they didn't just come to ask a lot of questions then go away again with no thoughts about returning." He stood up, walked half the length of the parlour, turned and walked back. "Alan, if your idea is right, then just maybe someone, somehow, let enough information slip in San Francisco as well as Tokyo, to make people believe there is a fortune hidden here on Emeraldia."

Alan nodded. Ford Courtland watched Frank's pacing without moving away from the front window, or interrupting. Frank went on speaking.

"If these people think someone might know something, they'll kill to find out. They've already proved that point. They killed the Commissioner. But by now they would have killed us too, except that they don't think we know anything."

"We don't," said Alan.

Frank stopped pacing and looked keenly at his friend. "But suppose they thought we *did?*"

Alan very slowly drew a rigid forefinger from left to right, from ear to ear, beneath his own chin. Frank nodded. He said, "Right. But they wouldn't believe you and I know anything; they've evidently already satisfied themselves we don't, otherwise they'd have visited us in the night the way they visited the Commissioner." Frank turned. "Mister Courtland; you're new here. You've just arrived . . ."

Courtland's eyes popped wide open. "Oh no," he said hastily. "Not on your damned life, Mister Chang. Look; I'm not a poor man. I don't give a damn about some old World War Two cache of stolen money. Even if the three of us found it, a half dozen governments would move in at once to file claims against it. As for being bait for some pirates, or whatever these people are, no thanks."

Frank smiled. "Mister Courtland, the word may already have got round. I can promise you one thing, anyone at all arriving on Emeraldia at this juncture is being watched and studied and checked-up on this very minute. Now, if those Japanese left the island a week ago, they had some reason for doing so. And then again, maybe they simply sailed out of sight until nightfall so the natives would believe they'd gone, then sailed back along one of the deserted beaches and are out there in the jungle right this minute."

Courtland's lean, mahogany face grew saturnine. "An awful lot of supposing," he said, glanced out the window, glanced back and made a quiet suggestion. "I'm not going to be bait for your theory, lads, but I'll give you a hand to this extent: If you'll come aboard tonight late, we'll up-anchor and cruise once around the island, in close, see what we can see, if anything, and be back at the anchorage before sunup."

Frank turned and winked at Alan as though to say he'd made a correct judgement concerning Ford Courtland. After that they parted, Courtland leaving those copies of wireless messages lying on Frank's coffee table. It was getting late and Alan said he'd have some work to do to get things prepared for his dinner guest. He made no sly allusion to that forthcoming interlude and Frank Chang didn't either. They both had something far more intriguing in mind. All Frank said was, "Be under the wharf by eleven-thirty; it'll take another half-hour or better to row out to the *Eleuthera*. By the way, there's an island in the Caribbean by that name. Did you know that?"

Alan hadn't known it. As he said, he couldn't possibly have cared less, either.

Frank waggled a finger under his nose as they parted. "I cared; you see, the Panamanian flag on the lugger, Courtland's story of being a ship-owner in the Central American trade, all fits very well with the name of the yacht. Made everything believable."

Alan grunted. "Damned clever these heathen Chinese!"

Frank laughed and went back into his bungalow while Alan headed up through the hot, steamy jungle towards his own dwelling. It was nearly five in the afternoon. Ford Courtland, looking grave and thoughtful, went strolling down towards Mama Kameha's restaurant-bar, about the only place on Emeraldia a stranger could go, unless it was back aboard the lugger, and he wasn't ready to do that just yet.

For Alan the time passed swiftly, which was usually the way when a person was doing something they enjoyed, such as preparing an intimate supper for two requiring all one's skill as a cook. Alan had possessed the penchant before arriving on Emeraldia. Afterwards, with the variety of foreign fish and vegetables available, he'd lost all cooking inhibitions and created dishes one could get nowhere except at his table. He liked food but more than that, he loved to cook.

As he explained it to Kathleen Scott when she arrived slightly before sundown, everyone has a spark of creativity; the vast majority of people live with it suppressed, either by their own inhibitions or by the demands of civilised, social living.

"Probably the greatest creative people the

world has ever known, were born, lived, and died and were buried without ever proving that they had genius. Furthermore, frustration is worse for people than any disease — it's a form of malignancy that slowly strangles initiative, and in the end actually kills people."

Kathleen smiled. "You're a cynic, Alan. A cynic and a rebel."

He let her help him pour wine, light candles, adjust the bamboo blinds to minimise an invasion of flying things attracted by the light, then he held her chair and as she sat down he said, "I am neither rebellious nor cynical, Kathleen; I simply felt stifled by civilisation, needed a place to be free — to be myself — to forget all the ersatz inhibitions. To create special dishes, to dine by candlelight with trade-winds on the roof. To live simply, unhurriedly and without a worry in the world."

She smiled. By candlelight her eyes seemed dark and inviting. "Is that how you live now?" she asked. "Don't you miss a lot that modern life offers?"

He shook his head slowly from side to side. "Television? The idea is wonderful. Regimented creativity, the most illicit kind, ruined television, Kathleen. Cars? Position? Wealth? I don't need any of them. Don't want them."

She considered him from amused eyes. "If everyone felt that way, Alan, Emeraldia would be overrun by now."

"No danger of everyone feeling that way,

Kathleen; people like you want wealth, social position, power, crowds, sophisticated existence. Percentagewise, love, there aren't actually very many dropouts from the modern maze. I happen to be one. On the other hand . . ."

"Yes, I know. You've already said it: I want wealth and comfort and social acccptance." She smiled, nodded at him and for a while simply concentrated upon her meal, which she said was delightful. Then she said, "Did you get the Commissioner's files for me?"

He looked blank, nor was he acting. "Good Lord, Katy, I forgot, but I'll trot down right after supper and bring them back."

"That would be putting you to . . ."

"Not a bit of it," he broke in, really chagrined. "It'll only take a moment. While you're having tea on the veranda and watching the moon rise over the ocean."

She seemed mildly piqued but only briefly. They resumed their meal. He got her a sprig of mint for her tea and fetched himself a second cup of coffee. A soft little high wind brushed palm fronds in the high trees making an audible whispering sound. The surf rose and fell back. The fragrance of flowers in the jungle behind Alan's bungalow kept the heavy, humid air fragrant. When the candles guttered and the bamboo shades moved it meant the breeze had dropped lower, but it was not strong. It never was, he said, not even when it rained, which it

123

very often did during this hot, sultry time of year.

"Of course when a typhoon comes by we get wind."

She was interested. "Has it happened often since you've been on Emeraldia?"

"Not often, but then, with a typhoon, it doesn't have to happen often. I've seen three of them. But of the lot only one braced the island. The others always seemed to bend away from us about thirty miles before they got here. I've stood atop the promontory with the villagers and watched them do that." He laughed. "It's like a last-minute reprieve."

"And the one that hit the island . . ?"

"Tore half the tin roof off Government House, played havoc with Frank Chang's shed, and toppled trees like matchsticks. Scared hell out of me, I don't mind admitting. But even so, it swept across the centre of the island and didn't hit Ibehlin head-on or of course the damage would have been much greater."

She looked at him. "And this is where you choose to live, Alan?"

He rose. They were finished with supper. "I'd say the chances of another typhoon hitting Emeraldia are approximately one out of thirty." He helped her up and steered her towards the front veranda. "Can you say your chances of being struck down by a car in London or New York are that good?"

There was a lovely moon, some fleecy dark

clouds, the sea was the colour of ancient jade, and pinpointed far out lay the lugger *Eleuthera,* clearance lights faintly visible.

He left her sitting there relaxed and comfortable, promised to be gone only a short while, and went trotting down the path towards Frank Chang's place — cursing his poor memory because now he had to waste perfectly good time.

Still, just the fact that they would examine the old files together might present an opening for him to question her.

That hadn't been precisely all he'd had in mind, though.

Well, he told himself in a scolding frame of mind as he hastened along, when a person gets too engrossed in one thing, it's hardly to be expected that he can, or will, be very much good in something else. However, if she was indeed Herbert Dentzel's wife or girlfriend, she wouldn't be interested in him anyway. He looked up at that idyllic moon, shook his head over the shameful waste, and slowed his pace as he approached the lighted residence ahead.

CHAPTER THIRTEEN

Conflicting Emotions

Frank had a surprise waiting. He admitted Alan then nodded about the files which Alan requested, and pointed to the coffee table, which was bare. "I don't see much of a future for you and me and Ford Courtland with MI5 or the C.I.A. Remember the copies of those wireless messages Courtland put there? Well, they are gone."

Alan looked blankly at the offending teakwood table. The only thing resting upon it was a half-empty tea cup. He tried hard to think back. He recalled seeing Courtland place the messages on the table but he couldn't remember whether, when Courtland departed, he'd taken them with him or not.

"Are you sure they were there, Frank, didn't Courtland take them with him?"

"No. In fact, I re-read them after you chaps left and before I went down to the sheds. That's where I left them. Right there on that damned table."

Alan went to a chair and sank down. "Very nice," he muttered. "We'd better hope Courtland had a change of mind and returned to get them."

Frank said glumly, "I'll get those old files for you," and left the room.

Alan lit a cigarette, eyed the table, turned to also glance at the door and windows, then blew smoke at the ceiling. If the pseudo Ford Courtland had got the copies of those messages he would know, not only that Frank and Alan were aware of his deceit, but he'd also know who the real Ford Courtland was.

That really didn't dismay him very much. The impersonator, big and powerful though he was, whether he knew it or not, was a prisoner. Everyone on Emeraldia was to some extent a prisoner. The nearest island was much farther than a man could paddle a canoe, and excluding the lugger *Eleuthera*, there was only Captain Voermann's monthly visit to succour those wishing to leave.

Alan's thoughts about Kathleen were different. If Dentzel had burglarised Frank's bungalow, had got those messages and knew now his impersonation was finished, wouldn't he have told his accomplice — if she was his accomplice — and wouldn't she have acted differently towards Alan at dinner?

He was still trying to puzzle this through when Frank returned carrying a dusty cardboard box full of old folders and musty papers. Alan arose to accept the box as Frank said, "I wish I'd sent that pile of junk to London with the rest of Mister Friday's possessions. I'm getting tired of lugging it out for everyone who visits the island." He dusted his hands, looked up at Alan and said, "I'm going down to Mama's place for a few drinks. I've got to know whether Dentzel stole those messages or if it was someone else. Alan, if it wasn't Dentzel I think we might not have too much to worry about — but *they* might have. I mean Dentzel and Scott. If whoever burglarised the bungalow gets an idea those two are also after some damned hidden cache, I have an idea they just might wake up with a bullet through the gizzard the way Mister Friday did."

Alan agreed with that, but he wasn't so sure he and Frank were in the clear. "If it was Dentzel, and if his ladyfriend knows anything about it, believe me I'll find out within the next couple of hours. If it *wasn't* Scott or Dentzel . . ." Alan looked squarely at Frank Chang. "Then I think maybe the lot of us had better take up residence on Courtland's boat for a while, because sure as hell those Japanese are back and this time they're calling the shots and making the rules."

Frank went as far as the porch with Alan. Afterwards, he struck off towards the heart of the village while Alan, without so much haste, returned to his bungalow where Kathleen was waiting. The last words they'd exchanged had to do with meeting at the dock before midnight.

Kathleen rose when she saw Alan coming. She protested at having made him go so far and bring back such a weighty box on his shoulder. He hadn't noticed the length of the hike nor the burden he'd carried.

They cleared his dining-room table so she could have plenty of room, then he made them both a rum highball while she started going through the old files. He watched her face; if she knew that Alan was aware she did not work for the Jenkins newspaper chain, she did not show it. He eventually arrived at the conclusion that if Dentzel were indeed the burglar who stole the messages from Frank's house, he hadn't told Miss Scott.

Whatever the man's purpose for not telling her might be, if indeed this were the case, as far as Alan could decide while he helped her go over the old files, she couldn't have been all that good an actress, not with genuine peril probably stalking her — if she knew it was stalking her.

He finally said, "Katy, whatever it is you're looking for isn't in those old copies of letters, directives, official letters dealing with trifles."

She raised her eyes from the paper in her hand, looking steadily at him. "Whatever I'm looking for, Alan? You make it sound as though I'm some kind of spy. I told you — I'm interested in a biography of Commissioner Friday. Anything about him interests me."

"How will you handle his death, in the biography?"

"Exactly as it happened: Murdered by a

person or persons unknown."

"You've got to do better, Katy. People don't want unsolved mysteries in books. You've got to at least come up with plausible theories."

"All right — suicide?"

"Did he get out of bed after shooting himself through the heart, hide the gun then climb back into bed?"

She dropped the paper and looked annoyed. "Alan, what are you trying to do? Your whole attitude, tonight, is different."

He wanted the worst way to tell her he knew she was not an employee of the Jenkins Syndicate, but instead he said, "Maybe save your life, Katy. Whoever killed the Commissioner is still wandering around with his gun."

She opened her eyes wide. "Alan, why would he want to kill me, and if he'd wanted to, why would he wait almost two months to do it?"

"On Emeraldia time isn't too important, Katy. It may have taken him this long to find out whatever he needed to know about you."

Now, the handsome face slowly closed towards Alan. The blue eyes got rock-hard and rock-steady. For a moment they simply sat there looking at one another, then she leaned with both arms atop the table and said softly, "Alan; what is it? What happened down at Chang's bungalow? You were different when you returned."

He glanced at his watch. It was slightly past nine o'clock. He'd originally feared he might be pressed for time but now he knew differently. He said, "I got to thinking on the way back here, Katy. You keep digging into the Commissioner's background, his private life, and although you may be serious about writing his biography, it occurs to me that someone else — the man who killed him — may not believe that's what you're interested in."

She sat perfectly still and continued to stare at him as though wondering whether to believe this was all he had in mind or not. After a while she slowly relaxed and smiled.

"What difference can it make what he believes, Alan?"

"Because, love, he didn't shoot Mister Friday just out of simple spite. There had to be something far more serious involved. And if this murderer thinks you are on the trail of whatever it was that made him pull that damned trigger, he's going to give you a dose of the same medicine. Just remember, Katy, no one hangs any higher for two murders than for one."

Her smile softened. "You're concerned for me. That's sweet, Alan. In fact *you're* sweet. As for the Commissioner's secret — if there was any such thing — the fact that he was killed over it means it went into the grave with him, doesn't it?"

He had to veer off; he also had to concede that she hadn't revealed anything, which meant that either she really didn't know very much, or she was a good actress. In either case he was frustrated. He emptied his highball and offered to get them both another one. She declined, kept smiling across the table and finally said, "Don't worry so much, Alan. If there was a secret it wouldn't be one any longer, would it; after all, look at the condition of these files. I'll wager half a dozen people have poured over them since Commissioner Friday's death."

That statement told him a little: She'd wanted to glance through the files to see if perhaps there might not be some clue the others who'd searched them, and who knew less than she knew, had missed. Of course that was a flimsy conjecture but it was substantiated by one thing he noticed: She went at once to the files dealing with the immediate post-war period on Emeraldia. That, to Alan, was more eloquent than anything he'd been able to draw out of her.

She finally finished with the files shortly after ten o'clock. Finally, too, she accepted his offer of another highball. They went out on to the veranda to have their nightcap. The moon was farther down than it had been when they'd visited the veranda earlier, and the jade-coloured sea was darker. That little wind had gone on, probably towards the China Sea, and off through the giant trees in a southerly direction could be seen the warm little scattered lights of the village.

It was quite warm; there would be no

noticeable cooling until an hour or two before dawn. She took a chair and quietly thanked him for a pleasant evening and a delightful dinner. She proposed a little toast.

"To your world, Alan, may it always remain exactly as it is now; exactly as you want it to be."

He smiled. She was very attractive in the starshine. He thanked her, made her promise she'd let him prepare another supper for her soon, then he said, "Katy, I hope you find it."

"Find what?"

"Whatever you're really looking for."

It was an ambiguous statement; he'd made it that way on purpose. While she struggled to determine which of several meanings he'd had in mind he watched her face in the quiet soft light. Eventually she said, "What am I looking for, Alan?"

"Oh; all those things we discussed earlier. Wealth, position, acceptance." He smiled. He had finally got the answer to what had been bothering him. If she'd been guiltless she'd have had these things he'd mentioned uppermost in mind. The fact that she was guarded now proved to his satisfaction that what she was seeking was perhaps right here on Emeraldia, and it wasn't any of the things he'd just mentioned. This knowledge also made him a little sad; she was a lovely woman, and whatever was at stake now would not take into consideration that she was a woman at all. After all, if something like twenty million dollars was secreted on Emeraldia, and if enough men knew this to be so, the killing of one beautiful woman wouldn't deter those men.

She finished the drink and he offered to walk back to the village with her. She half-heartedly protested but when she started down off the veranda and he went with her, it seemed to Alan that she was pleased to have him along.

The path was crooked but it was clear of obstructions. It passed a number of great trees from whose branches hung an endless variety of creepers. There were no such things as orchids on Emeraldia, although they would have flourished if anyone had ever thought to introduce them. There were other flowers with more perfume, and which were just as shade-loving and delicate. It was the fragrance of these that made a moonlight stroll for a man and woman very pleasant, very relaxing.

She said, "Alan, do come to London someday. I won't try to convert you, but it isn't good to hide from life too long. Will you do that?"

He took her hand as they walked. "Someday, perhaps. In exchange — will you return to Emeraldia?"

She smiled up at him without answering, but she leaned a little so that her hair brushed his cheek and they touched at hip and shoulder.

It was very pleasant. Not especially sensual, but only perhaps because neither of them was entirely free of other more perplexing thoughts, as well as being past the age for violent emotions involving virility, because Emeraldia was a place that would ordinarily arouse people.

They paced slowly along without saying any more until, near where the path skirted the dry coconuts and the fragrance of flowers was overcome by the other smell, he said, "The tragic part of a life on an atoll is that time inexorably passes, just as it does anywhere else. Katy, if I ever come to visit you in London, or if you ever return to Emeraldia, neither of us will be the same as we are tonight, will we?"

She squeezed his fingers. "You're getting sad before there's any reason, Alan." She stopped at the edge of the dusty road upon the far side of the drying coconuts, turned, stood on tiptoe and kissed him full on the mouth. Then she dropped down, smiled, turned and walked on towards the centre of the village alone.

CHAPTER FOURTEEN

A Boat Ride

Frank was impatiently waiting in the little boat beneath the dock. As Alan stepped down into the craft Frank said, "You're on time but I had my doubts about that."

Alan hefted a paddle without speaking. They pushed clear and headed across the glassy lagoon, invisible once they got a hundred yards from shore because the moon was behind a fat, dark cloud. Alan couldn't quite shake his melancholy. Frank, eyeing him now and then, wisely did not intrude.

They had a goodly distance to traverse but at least until they passed the natural shoals, which formed a breakwater for the bay, there was no opposition to their course from the sea. Afterwards there was; they had to make constant corrections to keep the craft pointing towards the red and green clearance lights on ahead that looked no larger up close than they'd looked from the shore.

They were still some distance off when they heard a man's soft call up ahead and Frank grunted something about Courtland keeping a watch posted. When they finally got alongside Courtland himself was there to welcome them aboard while a stalwart, unsmiling blond man took the line from Alan to make it fast to a small capstan.

There was a light showing from the below deck cabin whose small, oblong windows were only a foot or so above deck-level. They wordlessly followed Ford Courtland into the cabin and he mixed them all a drink, motioned them to chairs and said, while he drew a paper from a pocket, "Rewarding day, gentlemen." He held the paper aloft. "This thing cost me four hundred dollars."

He stepped to a table, sat, looked at his visitors then said, "What went wrong, you two look like you've been gazing into an open grave."

Frank spoke first. "Did you by any chance return after we three met at my place, and take the copies of those wireless messages you left on the table there?"

Courtland looked long at Frank, divined what had occurred and leaned back. "Gone?"

Frank nodded. "Gone."

"Why in the hell didn't you put . . . ?"

Frank interrupted sharply. "Whatever I should have done I didn't do. That much is water under the bridge. The point is — I have no idea who got into my cabin, nor why they'd choose this particular day for it, and stole those messages."

"Changes things," growled Courtland, and when that unsmiling, stalwart seaman poked his head in Courtland nodded almost absently at the man. "Shove off, Jack. Take the course we discussed earlier. No running lights." The seaman withdrew. Courtland looked sternly at Frank. "You have an idea who burglarised your place, Mister Chang. Dentzel, the woman, or some third party presently unknown to us."

"Not the woman," put in Alan. "She was with me having dinner."

Courtland nodded over that. "Dentzel then?"

Neither Chang nor Barton answered. Courtland, as though recalling something, touched the paper he'd formerly shown them. "Four hundred dollars worth of interesting information here," he said, but now the exultation that had been in his voice before, was lacking. Now, he sounded almost bleak.

"I'll tell you what Commissioner Friday died about, and what everyone is searching for." Courtland paused, read a few lines from the message under his hand, then spoke again, quoting the message. "Between 1942 and 1944 an estimated seventy million dollars was taken from public and private sources by the invading Japanese, of which less than ten million was afterwards accounted for." Courtland paused to look up. Frank and Alan were staring at him. He then said, "A dozen leads respecting the balance of this loot, mostly in cash and to a lesser extent in gold, have over the intervening quarter century proved worthless. Among captured Japanese documents found on Okinawa by U.S. forces after the war was a deathbed statement by one Akira Yamamoto stating that seven million in gold bars was sent to Japan by way of New Guinea."

Alan repeated the name. "Akira Yamamoto."

Courtland looked at him. "You know the name?"

"It's on a grave at the old hospital site in the centre of our island."

Courtland smiled. "Fine. Now we're getting somewhere. You see, that airplane never reached New Guinea. I've got the information right here. It did not reach Japan either. Gentlemen; seven million dollars worth of gold bars is one hell of a lot of solid, dead weight. If that aircraft went down at sea — that's the end of it unless flight records of the Imperial Japanese Air Force can give us a fix on the course taken, and even then without knowing where the damned thing fell into the sea we're still lost. I've got friends pouring over U.S. combat records to see if a Jap transport aircraft — it couldn't have been anything smaller for that load — was shot down on the date and upon the approximate course we're interested in. But this is going to take months; there were thousands of combat missions flown between 1942 and 1944."

Frank held up his hand. "Wait a minute: If some Japanese are already searching on Emeraldia, wouldn't it seem reasonable that they've already done all this spade work?"

Courtland nodded. "It would." He flicked a glance at Alan. "It would also mean that your theory about why Commissioner Friday was killed might be very close to the truth. But — how much did he know, and how did he find it out?"

Alan straightened in his chair, no longer feeling as melancholy as he'd felt before, his mind turning now to a subject equally as intriguing as his thoughts about Kathleen Scott. "Those three Japanese who visited the island some years back; the ones who had been stationed at the Jap evacuation hospital."

Frank and Courtland continued to stare at Alan for a bit, then Courtland nodded. "All right; it will probably cost me another four hundred dollars to find out their names but we've gone this far."

Frank said, "I'll make a wager: Your impersonator knows those names. He and his ladyfriend also must know a lot more, which probably means they've also done a lot of spade work on this affair."

Courtland looked drily at Alan. "Except for squeamishness on the part of some of us I'd have that information by now."

Alan ignored the thrust. "Listen to me for a moment: Those Japanese will kill. We know that. There is more money in that cache than anyone could spend. Suppose we invite Kathleen and Dentzel out to your boat, Mister Courtland, and put the cards on the table.

140

Share and share alike."

Frank fidgeted in his chair and Ford Courtland screwed up his face in hard thought. Alan's idea was both sudden and revolutionary to the others, but as he now said, "Everyone is going off on tangents in this mess — except the Japanese. Unless something is done, Commissioner Friday will only be the first casualty. Personally, I'm a lot less concerned over some gold bars than I am over my life. I think everyone else would feel the same way, including Dentzel. And you can damned well bet the Japs are watching the island. Frank; if they got those messages off your table, it's the same as signing Dentzel's and Kathleen Scott's death warrant. I said it once before tonight and now I'll say it again: You can't hang any higher for two — or five — murders, than you can for one."

Courtland got up and went to a small bar to freshen his drink. As he turned, asking if the others would like more ice, more mix or more liquor, that blond seaman poked his head through the doorway again and said, "Better come on deck, Mister Courtland."

All three of them went on deck. The *Eleuthera* had made her way around the southerly promontory to the uninhabited, rocky side of Emeraldia where birds lived by the thousands in little pock-marks in the cliffs, but otherwise there was little life at all. Most of those parapets were behind them and the island's coastline was dropping gently towards a gritty beach dotted with refuse washed up out of the sea. The blond seaman had a companion on the bow who pointed inland as Courtland, Frank and Alan appeared.

But it wasn't what they saw, for there was nothing to see, no light, no clearing, no movement. It was an identifiable scent being carried southerly, out to sea, from somewhere in the rain-forest.

"Cooking," said the seaman, still pointing inland. "Someone up there is cooking fish."

Courtland sniffed, then turned. "Any natives live on this side of the island?"

Frank shook his head and strained to see past the darkly impenetrable jungle growth where that fire had to be. "No. They can't grow anything here — too rocky, and the beaches are usually awash at high-tide so they can't launch their boats."

"Someone is in there," said Courtland, gazing towards the land. He turned to the unsmiling, blond seaman. "Get us out of here, Jack. No sense in having them see us."

The *Eleuthera* wallowed in wide troughs for a few moments longer, then the deck vibrated underfoot from a powerful, muted pulse and the vessel settled to her onward course.

Frank, silent for most of this period, leaned upon the rail and watched the island's physiognomy subtly change as they beat their way on around to the westerly curve, and here there were no beaches at all because the surf pounded up to the very edge of some dense, mangrove-type of wiry, spiny brush. Courtland and Alan strolled over to ask if Frank knew any area back there which would be suitable for someone to pitch a camp. He nodded.

"Several clearings, several springs. What bothers me is how they got here and where their boat is. It doesn't seem very likely they'd commit a murder here and expect to take away a ton or more of dead weight without having a way off the island close at hand."

Courtland was inclined to dismiss that. "Probably hidden up some little estuary."

Frank looked round with an ironic smile. "You saw the south side of the island. You're now seeing the west side of it. There's not a place anywhere along here where the sea wouldn't pound a boat to pieces at high-tide."

Alan, watching Frank's face, said, "You're thinking they've got some natives helping them?"

"I'm thinking they've sure as hell got *someone* helping them. Someone who either is hiding with the boat out at sea, or else who is guarding the boat for them among the fishing villages on the other side of the island."

Courtland suddenly made a decision on Alan's earlier suggestion. "Strength in numbers," he said. "I suppose we're going to have to bring Dentzel in with us."

Frank shrugged. "I only hope that is enough."

Courtland smiled. "It won't have to be, gentlemen. I can wire for a flying boat and some additional men. 'Can have them here by morning."

That was a cheerful idea. Frank lost a little of his gloom. He asked if Courtland owned a gun; the answer was that he had several on board, pistols and rifles. Frank then said he owned a pistol. Alan looked mildly pained; he didn't own any kind of a weapon. Courtland could provide him with one. He also asked for an opinion about importing some armed men from New Zealand or Australia.

Neither Frank nor Alan were keen on this, at least not when it was initially suggested, so the three of them returned to the below deck cabin to finish their highballs and digest what they'd come upon.

One thing was fairly certain; that had to be those Japanese back there in the jungle. It was difficult to imagine it might be someone else, unless, as Frank dryly said, there were more treasure-seekers around than anyone knew about.

By the time the *Eleuthera* returned to her anchorage a plan-of-sorts had been worked out. Ford Courtland wasn't altogether delighted because it did not include calling in armed aid just yet, but on the other hand it did involve bringing Dentzel and Kathleen Scott to the lugger in the morning, and that at least was a temporary diversion, and it also involved

144

making a very careful expedition into the jungle with as many local natives as Frank felt he needed and could trust, to have a look at whoever was living back there.

Later, unless something unforeseen occurred, they could bring in professionals and make a real manhunt of it.

Frank and Alan left the *Eleuthera* at four in the morning and rowed wearily back to the dock, making it one last time without being noticed, but they were also so exhausted they both headed straight for home and bed. It hadn't only been a fruitful, exciting night, it had also been a very tiring one.

CHAPTER FIFTEEN

A Conference

Frank appeared on Alan Barton's veranda at nine o'clock looking fresh enough but unsmiling. Alan was having a cup of coffee. Frank, more of a tea drinker, agreed to sit a moment and came inside. He had already seen Dentzel and had asked him to ride out to the lugger with him. Frank said he'd suggested, just for an outing, that Dentzel invite Kathleen Scott along. They were all to meet on Frank's dock in a half-hour. Frank had a motor launch; this time they wouldn't use paddles because this time when they went out to the lugger they wouldn't care who saw, or heard, them.

Alan asked if anything else was new. Frank shook his head. "Only a little tingling sensation I've got between my shoulder-blades every time I'm in my house, or each time I turn my back to the bush."

Alan didn't smile. He got Frank's tea, got himself a re-fill on the coffee, sat where he could see the sand and surf just beyond the thin fringe of giant trees beyond his veranda, and said, "Do you actually believe Emeraldia has seven million dollars worth of gold bars buried on it, Frank?"

Chang skirted a direct answer. "I'll tell you one thing, Alan, buried here or not some people certainly believe that gold is here, and that can be just as fatal as far as we are concerned. I wish to hell they'd find it and go away, or not find it and go away. That goes for all of them, not just the Japanese." Frank sipped tea, put the cup down and lit a cigarette. "I asked around among the people in the sheds, the warehouses and the drying grounds, trying to find out if there were any rumours, or if there was any actual knowledge, of strangers camping in the southwest bush."

"And you didn't find anything out."

"No."

"Your employees are town-natives, Frank. I doubt if two-thirds of them have ever set foot in that part of the island."

Frank nodded. "True, but the villagers on across the hill never go there either." Frank looked at Alan with a quizzical expression. "No one knows who is back there in the forest. But I had hoped someone might have glimpsed a Japanese slipping about on the outskirts of Ibehlin. No one has, of course, because a Japanese on Emeraldia would certainly be news worth passing along."

"All that proves is that the Japs are very careful."

Frank put out his cigarette and arose. "I wish I knew there were only four of them. It could get sticky if we went barging into their hideout and it turned out to be ten or twelve." He was speaking casually now, and he looked into Alan's empty cup then said, "Come on; our friends — or whatever they are — will be waiting at the dock." He turned suddenly and brought forth a little flat, ugly pistol from beneath his coat. At Alan's look of surprise Frank smiled.

"Take it, put your coat on and it won't show in your waistband." Frank opened his own cloth coat to show a second pistol. "Feels odd, I'll admit, but since everyone else will probably be carrying them we might as well do so too, eh?"

Alan held the gun and looked down at it with an expression of genuine distaste, then, as Frank's voice turned impatient, Alan shoved the gun into his waistband, got his coat and followed Chang out of the bungalow.

It wasn't hot yet although there was plenty of promise that the heat would come. In fact, there was a benign little wind coming in off the sea as the two men skirted round the drying area and angled past the sheds where that asthmatic old donkey-engine was noisily keeping the conveyor belt moving. Frank's foreman, a large, genial, rather dusky man threw them a wave from the shade of the shed and Frank looked rueful. "I think if the world came to an end he'd still find something to lean upon in the shade to watch it happen."

Kathleen Scott and Herbert Dentzel were

waiting as Frank had prophesied. Kathleen was in excellent spirits and Dentzel, whom Alan hadn't seen much of lately, appeared only slightly more subdued than he'd acted when he'd initially arrived on Emeraldia. It was quite possible Dentzel's spirits were taking a beating over his inability to find what he'd come for.

Still, as they stepped down into Frank's motor launch, it was Dentzel who produced four tins of beer from Mama Kameha's place, and proceeded to open them with a wicked pocket-knife and pass them around. For Alan it was a bit early, but as the fake Ford Courtland said, it was, after all, only beer. Alan drank; not because it was only beer, but because he felt distinctly uncomfortable thinking ahead to the confrontation shortly to ensue.

Frank was mostly silent on the ride out. When they were fairly close Dentzel said he'd been deceived by the distance, that the *Eleuthera* was considerably larger than he'd thought. He also acted as though he were beginning to have some rough-edged thoughts. He turned to Frank.

"This chap may resent a delegation dropping in on him. Or have you by any chance cleared it in advance?"

"He's expecting us," replied Frank, beginning to make the large turn which would bring their launch alongside. Three men were on the *Eleuthera*'s deck, two prepared to lend a hand, the third man standing up there tall and lean and unsmiling.

They drew in close, were prevented from abrasively rubbing by thick strips of car-tyre rubber, and came aboard the *Eleuthera* one by one. The only time Ford Courtland spoke was when Kathleen Scott, taking his hand, smiled upwards and said, "It's a frightful intrusion, I'm afraid."

Courtland smiled. "Hardly that. Please go into the cabin, I've set out tea."

He herded them all ahead of him. The deck cabin was rather spacious, as a matter of fact, but only because the lugger was broad-beamed which gave more width for inboard room. Still, with five people in it, and with the four men all being average size or better, it seemed slightly full. Courtland waved them all to seats. He had fixed things for tea at the table. Now he asked if anyone would care for a cup. Kathleen would, but evidently only because she wished to be polite. She and Ford Courtland had a cup. By that time it was painfully obvious this was no social visit. Courtland took his time, but when he was ready he smiled frostily, looked the impersonator squarely in the eye and said, "Why in the devil did you have to pick the name Ford Courtland; why couldn't you have just claimed to have been John Smith or Bill Jones?"

For five seconds it was so quiet in the cabin it was possible to hear water lapping against the hull. Everyone in the cabin was regarding Herbert Dentzel and he was studying Ford

Courtland through narrowed lids, his grey gaze steady, appraising, bleak.

Courtland sipped tea, finished, turned to put the cup aside and turned back to meet that bleak grey stare. "It's no longer any secret — Mister Herbert Dentzel. It might have remained one, though, if I hadn't appeared, because of that useless old wireless on the island. But Mister Dentzel, I am convinced you'd never have left Emeraldia with the cache even if you'd found it."

For the first time since he'd been stripped of his false identity Dentzel spoke. "No? Do you think you could have stopped me?"

Courtland shook his head. "I wouldn't even have tried to stop you, old man."

"Who are you?" demanded Dentzel, and as though he'd anticipated this question — which of course he had —the genuine Ford Courtland picked some papers off a small sideboard, leaned and placed them squarely in front of Dentzel. "Now do you see what I mean when I said you should have picked someone else to impersonate?"

Courtland touched Kathleen's shoulder. "More tea, my dear?"

She shook her head without speaking, her face white, her eyes large, round and troubled. Courtland patted her lightly, muttered something about there being nothing for her to fear, and smiled icily into the upraised face of Herbert Dentzel, who now knew whose boat he was on, and why Courtland has told him he should have selected another identity.

Dentzel matched Courtland's icy smile with one just as devoid of genuine humour. "It was a chance I had to take. I thought it was a good one, too, because when I asked a friend to look you up in London, she wrote me that you hadn't lived at that address for years."

Courtland nodded. "Never trust the judgement of a woman. I haven't lived there for years — I've lived on this side of the world. But that's neither here nor there, Mister Dentzel. Please clarify one thing for me, then we can get down to business."

"What thing?"

Courtland looked down at Kathleen. "Is she your wife, your ladyfriend, your partner — what?"

Alan and Frank waited for the answer. It didn't really surprise them when it came. It disappointed Alan a little, made him mildly regretful and unhappy, but it didn't break his heart; didn't even fracture it.

"She is my wife."

Courtland said, "Fair enough. Now all that is over with, suppose we get down to business. Mister Dentzel, what, specifically, are you seeking on Emeraldia?"

Herbert Dentzel looked as though he might spring to his feet. "Get the hell down off that high-horse, Courtland," he snarled. "Don't try running this like it was an inquisition with you

152

as grand master. You know as well as I do, what I was after."

"All right. I'm sorry if I gave an impression that offended you," said Courtland, "but as you'll soon find out, this is no meeting just to humiliate you. Tell us how you knew there was a cache on Emeraldia."

"I didn't know it was on Emeraldia. I knew it was somewhere in this general area. I was a PT-Boat skipper after the war out here. We used to hear all manner of wild tales, but this particular tale never varied. Later, I did a little checking." Dentzel shrugged thick shoulders. "You can imagine the rest. When I discovered how much bullion could be involved I made finding it a hobby. Then last year we decided to make it a business." He looked from his wife to Alan, to Frank, to Ford Courtland. "How did you fellows find out about the cache?"

"We didn't," Alan said, and proceeded to explain what had happened, including the boat trip around the island the night before, the discovery on the far side of the island, and the conclusion he and Frank had come to with Courtland.

Dentzel was not as surprised as Frank and Alan had thought he might be. He said, "Yeah; I'm not surprised about the Japs. While Kathleen and I were researching this affair we kept coming across the name Yamamoto. He was administrative officer at the evacuation hospital on Emeraldia. There were two other

153

officers too, both Jap surgeons. The odd thing is that all three of those men are dead — shot to death without apparent reason, in Japan."

Alan offered smokes around, held a match for Frank and himself, the only ones to light up, and afterwards said, "Did those three men visit Emeraldia, by any chance?"

"They visited all right. As you know, the younger Yamamoto is buried here."

Alan nodded. "Getting back to his father and the others — was there a connection between their shootings and the shooting of Commissioner Friday?"

"There was. At least Yamamoto knew where a cache of Japanese loot left over from World War Two was hidden. Probably the other two men also knew. Now, from here on it's all guesswork. I think whoever those Japs are who also know about the cache, must have extracted their information from Yamamoto or one of the others before murdering them. They then killed Friday probably because they thought Yamamoto, on his visit here, might have told the Commissioner. Personally, I think the Commissioner knew where the cache was. I also think Yamamoto or one of the Japs who came here on the visit with him, must have told the killers Friday knew, perhaps while being tortured. In any case, Friday was killed, Yamamoto and the others who knew where that cache is, were also killed. So now the knowledge is second-hand." Dentzel lit one of his own cigarettes, looked keenly around and said, "One thing, lads: Why haven't the Japs taken the cache away before now?"

Frank nodded softly. "I was going to ask you that."

"Because — I'm only guessing now — because the place where that stuff was buried twenty-five years ago on this damned tropical island can no longer be identified by the landmarks which have completely changed since those days."

Frank blew smoke, thought a moment, then nodded. That was very possible. In fact, it didn't ordinarily take twenty-five years for the tropical jungle to completely renew itself; it sometimes took only five or six years.

They sat looking at one another throughout a long moment of silence before Courtland said, "Mister Dentzel; the purpose in bringing you out here this morning was to suggest some kind of partnership. The five of us against those Japanese, and incidentally, they already know who you are, and I'd hazard a guess they also know who I am too. In any case, for mutual help and protection, a partnership is proposed."

CHAPTER SIXTEEN

The Strategy

Dentzel's acceptance of the proposed partnership was based on the same thought that Courtland had once put forth — Seven million dollars, or even a part of that amount, was enough for everyone.

Frank said, "And about those Japanese . . ."

Dentzel, still with the initiative, nodded. "You know, if they hadn't been so damned deadly, going round murdering people to prevent others from learning about the cache, we could probably have made an arrangement with them; taken them in as partners too. Of course that's out now, so I suppose we're all enemies."

Frank wasn't very interested in abstractions.

He said, "I'm concerned with who they might murder next, Mister Dentzel. Not who they have already murdered."

Courtland explained about the proposed stalk through the jungle to the place where the Japanese had their secret camp. Kathleen, a silent observer up to this point, now said, "You'll get killed." She looked anxiously at them. "Couldn't the natives be — ?"

"No natives," broke in Frank flatly. "They aren't warlike at all. If those Japanese wanted to they could cut a party of natives to pieces. I'm not going to stand for anything like that."

Courtland returned to his favourite suggestion once again. "We can have armed men flown in, you know."

Dentzel squashed that. "There are already too many who know the cache might be on Emeraldia. Fly in some New Zealanders or Aussies and pretty soon it'll be in every newspaper in the world and they'll be dropping in on us a hundred at a time." He rose from the table and leaned upon it looking squarely at his wife. "No need to fret, Katy. We always knew there would in all probability be others, didn't we?"

"But not murderers, Herb."

Dentzel shrugged his heavy shoulders, still smiling. "Any time there is this kind of money involved, love, you can bet your blessed boots there'll be murderers about, even if they never killed anyone before in their lives." He shifted his attention to Alan, to Frank, to Ford Courtland, still wearing that little tough smile. "We don't know where the damned cache is — but the Japs do. Now, whether we want trouble with the Japs or not . . ." Courtland was slowly nodding so Dentzel didn't bother finishing his obvious remark. Instead, he straightened up off the table. "How about your crewmen?" he asked Courtland. "You said four Japs, but are you sure there are only that many?"

No one was sure. No one, in fact, knew anything about the Japanese except what had been said by the natives. Courtland was of the opinion, although he hadn't told his two crewmen anything yet, that as soon as they learned how much bullion was involved and that they'd be entitled to a share, they would be eager to join in, but he also made a point well worth consideration.

"If the wartime Japanese melted that bullion into bars, there are still going to be a dozen governments putting in claims — providing of course that we unearth the stuff."

Alan, who had been quiet and thoughtful for a long while, suddenly said, "This grave with the brass plaque — it wouldn't be buried there, would it?"

No one heeded Courtland's remark when Alan spoke up, instead they all looked at him. It was increasingly apparent that with the possible exception of Kathleen Scott Dentzel, the gold-fever was taking hold.

Frank shook his head. "That's not our worry right now. If we dug into the grave and found gold bars there, you can bet all we'll find is that if the Japs know it's there, they'll also be watching the site day and night." He paused for that to sink in, then said, "First, we've got to neutralise the Japanese. Secondly, we can go treasure hunting."

Courtland agreed, and for a man who had very recently declined to be bait, his next remark was rather daring. "Mister Chang, you know the island's interior better than any of the rest of us. You lead us to their camp."

Frank scowled, obviously not enthusiastic about this, and yet he couldn't have expected anything else, so he had to be prepared for the suggestion. He said, "They are watching the village. My guess is that while several of them are trying to re-locate the cache, at least one of them is also keeping an eye on us. We'll either have to catch that one, or else try slipping up on their camp in the night, and frankly, going through that damned jungle at night gives me the chills."

Dentzel had a suggestion. "Let's go back," he said to Frank and Alan, "ease out of the village casually and see if we can't at least locate the spot where that watcher is hiding."

Frank had a better idea. "For this the natives will be better. Those Japanese wouldn't think much of seeing islanders poking about in the bush, but they'd surely think something was odd if you and Alan and I suddenly started poking about." Frank rose, his decision made. "I've got a dozen good men working for me who can be depended upon to find that spy."

Alan rose. Everyone was on their feet except Kathleen. She eventually, somewhat reluctantly, also stood up. It was apparent that although she'd gone along with her husband, now that there was real peril in the offing, her enthusiasm was waning. Still, she said nothing as they all went back on deck where a boiling sun had turned the sea a hot, pale colour, like clean steel.

A few clouds floated overhead. Emeraldia looked cool and shady and very dark green in the near distance. Alan stepped up beside the girl and leaned down to say, "Paradise has finally come foul of civilisation. For my part it would be just fine if the Japanese have already got the bullion and gone."

She nodded without looking up. Courtland was telling the others as soon as he'd sounded out his crewmen he'd up-anchor, sail into Ibehlin Bay and drop anchor closer to the wharf, then he'd come ashore and meet them all at Mama Kameha's bar. By that time, he hoped, Frank would have completed arrangements for his natives to start their search.

After that everyone but Courtland piled back into Frank's launch. As they cast off and started churning back across the glassy sea, Dentzel turned to Chang with a steady stare and said, "I made a mistake in assuming that old wireless set on the island was my best friend."

Frank wasn't thinking about Dentzel at all, but he said, "It doesn't matter now, Mister Dentzel. But Courtland was right about one thing: You should have taken some other identity."

"No. You'd have helped the Commissioner's nephew, not a total stranger."

Frank didn't reply to that. Neither did Alan

160

who was sitting in the bow staring towards the island through squinted eyes. Even Kathleen was no longer concerned with the deception, and eventually Dentzel himself stopped considering what had happened back there on the *Eleuthera*.

Up ahead was a staggering fortune. Regardless of the ultimate disposition of it — if they actually unearthed it — there would be a finder's-fee. Dentzel said, "Ten per cent, maybe twenty per cent, is still one hell of a lot of money split seven ways."

They parted at the wharf, Frank and Alan heading for Frank's bungalow, the Dentzels heading for Mama Kameha's place. The village was somnolent; the hot-time was upon the island. A few scrawny chickens scratched in the dust near the drying-grounds and some dusky children were playing some game involving peeled sticks in the shade near the sheds, but otherwise, except for a tinny echo of music coming from a thatched-roof house not far away, the village was drowsily unconcerned.

Frank reiterated his earlier remark about not getting his natives involved. He seemed now to be having second-thoughts about even using them to locate the Japanese who was probably hiding somewhere on higher ground, keeping an eye on the village, perhaps in the forest up behind Government House, since that was the only elevation close enough yet high enough for someone to see the entire village from.

Alan asked what the alternative was and Frank admitted there was none. Villagers came and went, and so far the secretive Japanese hadn't molested them, so obviously they didn't consider native islanders as any danger. Of course they'd made a point of avoiding them, but as Frank said now, that wouldn't be hard since the villagers didn't go to the southwest area of the island, anyway, and one spy, concealed and wary wouldn't encounter much difficulty avoiding detection since the islanders had no idea he would be out there.

"And supposing he isn't out there," said Alan. "After all, we only have the word of two fishermen from the north-side villages that any Japanese were here at all."

Frank looked wry. "He's out there all right. Who else slipped down here and stole those copies of the messages? It sure as hell wasn't a native; it wasn't you or me or the Dentzels." Frank consulted his watch. "I'll go down to the bar and round up some of the people I want to do the searching for us. When you see Courtland's lugger come into the bay hike on down. We'll have a cold beer."

Alan went up through the gloomy path to his own residence, showered, changed his clothing, deliberately left the ugly pistol on his dresser and made himself a light lunch, then went out onto the veranda to sit and think. He fell asleep out there instead.

For Frank the visit to Mama Kameha's bar

was no journey of joy; he knew the people who worked for him, liked them, and even if he hadn't it still would have been difficult for him knowingly to send them into danger through deceit. On the other hand if he told them what was happening on their island, explained about the cache, within hours that information would spread all over the island and the blithe natives would start searching too, which without doubt would result in some of them running foul of the armed and deadly Japanese.

He consoled himself as he picked out the men he wanted by telling himself that this was the best way to do what had to be done. He also felt that unless the Japanese were rooted out, sooner or later they would be found by natives out hunting, and there would be danger in that way too.

The trick, of course, was to explain that there might be a Japanese somewhere out at the back of the village in hiding, watching people, without saying too much about the reason for the spy being there. Fortunately, Frank had the trust of his people. As they sauntered out of the bar one and two at a time, they were willing to seek the spy without asking too many questions. Frank promised a cash reward to the finder.

It was dowdy, grey and shrewd Mama Kameha who came to Frank's table when the last native had departed, took a chair and said, "There is one thing unmarried men never un-

163

derstand, Frank — female intuition."

Frank smiled, a trifle uneasily because he'd known Mama Kameha most of his life, respected her shrewdness, and knew that now she was going to either scold him or ask some awkward questions.

"What are they going out into the bush to look for, Frank?"

"A Japanese," he said truthfully.

"Lost, hurt, sick . . . ?"

Frank glanced up as the Dentzels came through a rear door into the barroom. "You've got customers, Mama."

"Never mind my customers. They can wait. Frank . . . ?"

"I can't explain right now, Mama."

"All right; then I'll tell you something, Frank Chang: I may be old and fat but my hearing is still pretty good. There was talk a few days back about some Japanese visiting the fishing villages on the far side of the island. They asked a lot of questions about that old wartime hospital; about landmarks back there, things like that. Now you're involved too, aren't you?"

"Yes."

Mama Kameha leaned upon the table and shook her head at Frank. "Listen, whatever it is, don't let it bring trouble. You're always saying you want Emeraldia to stay as it is. Frank; don't let —"

He said shortly and swiftly, "Wait a minute! *I* didn't bring this mess to Emeraldia, Mama. All

I'm trying to do is get it settled so all these out-landers will go away."

"How, by sending the natives into the bush Jap-hunting? Frank, I can show you graves of natives who did that during the war. They weren't able to match the Japanese."

Frank looked barward where the Dentzels were sitting on benches with their backs to him. He shook his head in their direction as though disapproving of something about them. Then he said, "There is no other way to get these damned people off the island, Mama."

"Why don't you and Alan go Jap-hunting? At least you two would be better at it."

"Because we're the ones this Jap is watching. We've got to sit here like clay pigeons for him to watch while the natives locate his hiding place. Don't worry, I offered ten dollars to the man who sees him, and I gave strict orders no one is to approach him nor even act as though they'd found him. They are to find him — if they can — then report back to me this evening." Frank blew out a shaky breath. "I need a drink."

Mama Kameha made no move to get the drink. She studied Frank's troubled face for a while, then said, "I hope it works the way you've just said," then she rose and went padding across to her bar where she wordlessly waited on the Dentzels first, then mixed a high-ball and took it back to Frank's table, where she leaned down and said, "When it's over you're going to tell me what it was all about?"

"Of course I'll tell you."

Mama Kameha smiled. "Now you know what it is like to have people trust you; it's not just a matter of feeling good because they do, it's also being responsible for the things you tell them to do." She patted Frank's hand. "I'm one that trusts you."

Frank lifted the glass, sipped, watched the doorway until Alan came in looking rumpled and puffy-eyed from his nap, and put the glass down waiting for Alan to join him at the table.

It was by then four in the afternoon.

CHAPTER SEVENTEEN

The Bold Step

As Alan took the chair at Frank's table recently vacated by Mama Kameha he said, "The *Eleuthera* just dropped anchor off the dock. Courtland will no doubt be along in a few minutes." He saw the Dentzels up at the bar. "Poor Kathleen; about now she's wishing she'd never agreed to go along with him in this."

Mama Kameha brought Alan a gin and tonic. She looked to see whether Frank's drink needed freshening, it did. She took it away.

Alan asked if Frank had sent natives out. Frank nodded. "If anything happens to one of them . . ."

"Nothing will," exclaimed Alan, tasting his drink. "Emeraldians are the only people on earth who are by nature immune to real peril. I've seen it a hundred times. They swim with sharks, swing those big knives all day, concoct wine out of the damnedest vines, and nothing ever happens."

"Courtland's crewmen are joining us, I see," said Frank, and Alan leaned far forward to also gaze out the window. Frank was correct; Courtland and his two sailors, both large, stalwart men, were coming across the dock-area

167

towards Mama Kameha's place. Frank rose, gulped the fresh drink that had been set in front of him and said, "I'll go and head them off. We can't very well talk in here without starting all manner of rumours. You bring the Dentzels, Alan, and I'll take Courtland to my place."

Alan let Frank pass through the front doorway before approaching the Dentzels to say they would all meet at Frank Chang's bungalow. Kathleen nodded. She had half a lukewarm drink between both hands. She was rolling the glass forth and back making no attempt to drain it. Her husband nodded absently at Alan giving the impression of someone who had been through a bad afternoon. Alan could imagine what had been said between these two since Kathleen had made it plain enough on the boat that she was fast losing enthusiasm — if, indeed, she'd ever had any.

Alan said, "It will probably be worth the effort, Katy."

She looked at him. "Alan, those Japanese could kill us all."

"You had to know there would be some danger, Katy."

"No; as far as we knew no one else was looking for the cache on Emeraldia. We had no idea those Japanese would be here, ahead of us, in fact. We knew they were active in their own country, but we — I at least — didn't expect to run into them here. Alan, if we interfere they'll do the same to us they did to —"

"Katy, it is too late to back out even if we wanted to," said Alan. "They have been watching all of us. Since they have the copies of Courtland's messages they also know you and your husband are not what you said you were. No great amount of intelligence would be required for them to guess why you people are here. Even Frank and I, who live here, aren't above some suspicion although we've given them no reason to think we even know about the cache. At least, until quite recently, we haven't seemed to know." He patted her shoulder. "Come along to Frank's place, both of you."

They went. Dentzel wasn't perturbed whether his wife was or not, but he had never appeared the kind of person to frighten easily. Possibly the slight bulge under his jacket fortified his normal courage. In any event, Alan noticed it as they stepped up onto Frank Chang's porch.

Inside, Ford Courtland nodded curtly towards the newcomers and introduced his crewmen. The unsmiling blond man was named John Carter — Courtland called him "Jack." The other man, dark-eyed, pockmarked and thin-lipped, was named Fred Bates, but he had a Levantine look to him.

Frank nodded at the Dentzels, at Alan, and methodically poured tea into a number of cups on his teakwood table. "Any sign of my lads returning?" he asked Alan, not sounding as though he expected an affirmative answer.

Alan hadn't been watching out for natives. He said, as far as he knew, no one had returned to Mama Kameha's place yet.

Courtland looked at his watch and his two crewmen took cups of tea and seemed perfectly willing to be observers rather than participants for a while yet. Even when Courtland said his men were willing to join up, the seamen only nodded.

Katy brought up the topic Courtland had championed: Importing armed men to Emeraldia. She didn't act as though she expected the idea to be agreed to any more heartily now than it had been that afternoon on the lugger, but she looked a little desperate now. Alan, standing nearby, was sympathetic, but he was also silent because her husband said, "Too late, duck. I told you it was. We're on the move already."

Courtland, looking from husband to wife, and back again, had to nod agreement. "We'll be extremely careful," he assured her, with a little smile lifting the edges of his thin lips.

They were all armed with the exception of Alan. He noted that and felt slightly guilty about having left the gun up at the bungalow. Still, there couldn't be much need for the thing this evening and, beginning tomorrow, he'd wear it.

The sun hadn't been gone very long when

Frank was summoned to the door by his grinning shed-foreman, that somewhat soft and lazy individual whose hazel eyes seemed always to be seeking humour in whatever they saw. Alan went along in response to Frank's little nod of invitation.

The foreman said, "They find him." He looked at a wiry youth of no more than twenty or twenty-one who was standing there, white teeth glistening in a triumphant smile, hand extended. Frank dug out a note and lay it upon the extended palm. "Where?" he asked the youth.

"Got a platform in a tree. I seen him climbin' down. Except that he was movin' I'd have missed him. I got down in some bushes and waited. I followed him."

Frank frowned. "I told you not to."

The youth was undismayed. "Yeah. Anyway, I went behind him until he met another Jap, then they went off together and I come back to town."

The foreman, still grinning, said, "Be pretty simple thing, dig a boar-pit at the foot of his tree tonight. Tomorrow mornin' he fall in and you can have him." The grin widened a little. "Maybe cost two, three dollar is all. Dollar for me to supervise, dollar each for two fellers who'll make the pit. All right?"

Frank looked at Alan. "They're damned good at making those things. It's how they trap the wild pigs."

Alan was sceptical. "They'd better be damned good, Frank. That Jap isn't going to just come blindly along and drop into the thing — and what about the spearheads of sharpened bamboo they put down there?"

"No bamboo," said the foreman, smiling at Alan. "We make it so good no Jap will know it's there. For three, four dollars you can have . . ."

"Three," growled Frank, looking at the large native. "All right, but make it very, very good. This isn't a pig we're after."

"Sure. And after he's in there . . . ?"

"Don't go near the trap. Whatever you do don't poke your head over the edge. He'll have a gun. Come and let me know. You understand? Don't talk to him, don't look down at him, just come let me know he's in the pit."

The natives departed pleased, and animatedly talking. Frank accepted the smoke Alan offered him, lit it and looked after them. "That's what I was afraid of. You heard the kid say he'd followed that Japanese." Frank exhaled and wagged his head. "You tell them how to do something and they always have to try and go you one better. If one of them has to laugh down at that Jap we could have another killing."

They went indoors, explained what Frank had authorised, discussed the fact that their surmise concerning the spy was correct, then all had one stiff drink of Frank's liquor before Dentzel said, "Suppose he gets off a few shots when he's down in that hole, to let his friends know something has gone wrong?"

It was, of course, a possibility. Courtland's blond sailor had an answer. "Fred and I can go up there, get settled in the underbrush, and be on hand when he drops in to discourage anything like that." The other seaman nodded agreement.

There were no objections although Frank said he had doubts. He was blunt about it, too. "One mistake will blow the whole thing. It could also get someone killed."

The dark sailor, the one called Fred Bates, smiled at Frank. "There won't be any mistake, Mister Chang. As for anyone getting killed — don't worry about that. We got to have that Jap alive."

Frank looked at the sailor. He hadn't expected the man's viewpoint to be this astute. "Good luck," he said. "If anything goes wrong they'll be tipped off, and that could mean that they'd leave the island. You know what *that* means . . . they know where the cache is, we don't; if they leave there's a hell of a good chance we'll never find it."

They broke up shortly after this brief exchange but Alan lingered after the others had departed, to have a final smoke on Frank's veranda. Frank said, almost bitterly, "You and I should have gone up to dig that damned pit."

Alan looked surprised. "Why us? I've never dug a boar-pit in my life."

"Because I don't want anything to happen to a native. As for digging the pit — what could be so difficult about a six or seven foot hole straight down in the ground?"

"Work," responded Alan quickly. "Hard, hard work." He blew smoke, gazed up the quiet broad roadway of the village where there was no visible movement although it was still relatively early in the night, then he said, "I have a feeling Bates and Carter will be able to handle whatever comes up. I wouldn't worry about them if I were you."

Frank wasn't worrying about the pair of seamen. At least he wasn't worrying exclusively about them. He was worrying about everything; the Dentzels, Courtland, those two armed sailors, the natives. He was even worrying about the Japanese, and at least in this instance the anxiety seemed justified. He looked over at Alan, placidly enjoying his cigarette on Frank's porch and sniffing the fragrant night. "Whatever goes sour, Alan, Kathleen is going to hate the lot of us."

"She will anyway, Frank. At least she will providing her husband is hurt, or providing we don't find the cache, but once she's back in London with a little time to forget, it will pass." Alan smiled gently. "As far as I'm concerned I can stand a little dislike from all of them if we find the cache and if they all go away afterwards."

Frank seemed not to have heard. He said,

"Old Voermann's due the end of the week."

Alan stiffened. "Wait a minute, you're not thinking of inviting him to join in too, are you?"

"Of course not. I'm thinking of what might happen after — and *if* — we find that damned cache."

"What's Voermann got to do with it?"

Frank turned, looking very patient. "Alan, we can't call Auckland or Brisbane from Courtland's wireless to let people know some of that stolen loot has been recovered. We can't just divide it all up and let everyone sail away. Voermann can take some letters back and post them for us."

"You don't trust Courtland?"

Frank looked ironic about that, but his reply was patiently oblique. "I trust him; I just don't want to put him or anyone else, in the position of being tempted to do something rash, if we turn up with a hoard of gold bars."

Alan put out his cigarette and raised both arms to stretch while he yawned. "There's a flaw, Frank: Voermann won't be here before the end of this week. If we catch one of the Japs tomorrow, sweat some answers out of him, we damned well may have the cache before Voermann even arrives here, let alone before he can return and post any letters, which in turn wouldn't in all probability, get through the bureaucracies in Australia or New Zealand for another week or two."

It was true and Frank knew it. He wasn't happy about it, nor was he happy over feeling such distrust, but as he now said, it was beginning to look as though finding that cache might just be the first phase of their involvement.

He then ended it all up by repeating what he'd said privately to Alan upon other occasions since the affair had first come to light.

"I wish those damned Japanese had dropped that stuff in the sea, or had stacked it away on some other island."

"Emeraldia was perfect for hiding their cache," said Alan, and started down off the veranda. "It was such an insignificant, backward, unimportant place. Who would ever think of finding buried treasure here? Good night, Frank. You worry too much."

Frank watched Alan stride off up the little pathway leading out of the village towards his bungalow set apart on the edge of the palm-fringed beach. *Someone,* he told himself, had better worry, besides Kathleen, because if they trapped themselves a Japanese by morning, it wouldn't take very long before his friends knew what had happened, and after that no one would be wearing kid gloves any more.

CHAPTER EIGHTEEN

A Co-operative Prisoner

They caught the Japanese.

Frank was making his morning cup of tea when Bates and Carter, Courtland's sailors, stamped up on to his veranda with their captive. Frank admitted the three of them, gazed at the wiry alien, then said, "Tea?" It sounded ridiculous even to Frank, to the sailors it must have sounded worse because they both stared at him.

It was the Japanese who said in quite good English that he would like a cup of tea very much. He seemed as calm over his captivity as Bates and Carter seemed grim over it. Frank, studying the man, found him to be middle-aged, not very tall even for a Japanese, and either resigned or philosophical over being captured.

Frank led the way to his small kitchen, wordlessly poured three cups of tea — two of which were completely ignored by the seamen — and motioned for the prisoner to be seated. He took a chair with a slight hiss and a bow. Then he smiled up into Frank's face out of jet-black, small and shiny eyes.

"Very good, you catched me in hole. May I

ask why you do it?"

The unsmiling blond sailor, Jack Carter, stepped over and deliberately placed a small automatic pistol on the table. "Had it in his hip pocket. I unloaded it after we took it off him."

Alan Barton came to the veranda door. Frank called for him to come inside, then, with Alan looking round-eyed at the Japanese Frank sent him after the Dentzels, and at the same time he sent Courtland's dark sailor to bring his employer back too.

After only the expressionless blond man was left, excepting of course the small Japanese, Frank lit a cigarette, toyed with the automatic pistol then gazed at the prisoner. He hadn't answered the Japanese's question and obviously he wasn't going to answer it now.

He put the gun down very gently, waited politely for the prisoner to put down his tea cup, then he said, "Unfortunately the jungle changes every few years. After a quarter of a century nothing looks the same, does it?"

The Jap's eyes narrowed. He considered Frank for a moment, then said, "I understand. You know . . ." Frank nodded, Jack Carter straddled a chair watching the prisoner, and the Japanese softly smiled at Frank, ignoring the blond man. "You make a bad mistake."

Frank said, "*I* didn't fall into a boar-pit."

The Japanese hissed and smiled, then said, "If you knew why did you wait so long?"

"I didn't know there was a cache here on the

island," replied Frank, "if that's what you mean, until these other people came looking for it, but we heard about you when you visited the villages on the back of the island a couple of weeks ago. As for the cache — if you knew where it was, why haven't you taken it and gone?"

"You just said the jungle changes. That is the reason."

"Was it Yamamoto who told you it was here?"

Again the prisoner looked surprised, but he recovered as quickly as before, hiding the astonishment behind that genial smile. "Not Yamamoto."

"One of the others. I see. Why didn't you bring him with you; he would have known the place, I suppose." Frank knew perfectly well why the Japanese hadn't brought their informant; because they had murdered him as soon as he'd disclosed the whereabouts of the cache to keep him from telling anyone else where it was.

The Japanese only smiled this time, he did not speak at all. Shortly after this the Dentzels returned with Alan, slightly breathless, and they'd scarcely arrived before Courtland and the swarthy sailor also came along. The prisoner kept smiling, his obsidian eyes as unfathomable as black marble, his smile concealing whatever was in his mind. Ford Courtland astonished everyone by saying something in a quick, sing-song reedy language that erased the Jap's smile. He answered in the same sing-song language and Courtland poked fisted hands into trouser pockets, glanced at the others and said, "There are six of them, not four, but there are only four on the island. The other two are aboard a fishing boat lying several miles out to sea. They are in radio contact." He studied the prisoner a moment then said, "Well; we have several hours to find their camp and either bait the boat to us, or smash their radio. It will be that long before the other three finish their searching over at the old hospital site."

Jack Carter said, "If you know they're at the hospital site why can't we slip over there and catch them too?"

It was Frank who scotched that. "They would either see us coming or hear us before we even got close. And they might be anywhere within a mile of the site, we wouldn't know where they were." He asked Courtland to see if the prisoner would tell them where his companions were making their search. Courtland did this and the Jap answered in a quiet, short sentence that Courtland grimaced over.

"He said they widen their search-pattern a little each day; he isn't sure exactly where they'd be."

Dentzel came up with the most logical course of action. "All right, we know they aren't anywhere near their camp, so let's concentrate on finding that radio and smashing it."

Alan, watching the prisoner, saw the man's lips lift. The prisoner seemed pleased at this suggestion. Alan said, "We'd better take this one along as a shield. I've a feeling something isn't right."

Frank re-filled the captive's cup with tea. The middle-aged, wiry foreigner hissed and ducked his head in gratitude. Courtland snapped at him. The man, without losing his smile, answered back. Courtland's lean, dark face turned crafty and thoughtful.

"He says we couldn't find their camp, but I'm inclined to agree with Barton; that's not the point at all." He said something else in Japanese and this time the prisoner looked over the rim of his cup at Courtland, kept on smiling and made no attempt to reply. Courtland's face close down against the man. He withdrew both hands from his pockets.

Frank Chang, guessing the other man's intentions, intervened. "We'll take him along and we'll find the camp. I know that country over there."

Courtland was still glaring when he said quietly, "They've got their camp booby-trapped or something. I could get it out of him if you people would go outside for a moment." At Frank's swift look of dogged disapproval Courtland said, "Listen, Chang; these people wouldn't hesitate for a second doing much worse to you if the positions were reversed. I know. I've seen plenty of their handiwork in my time."

Kathleen, silent and standing back near the kitchen door, eased over beside her husband. The Japanese was looking steadily at her, his smiling eyes mere slits in a lined, mahogany countenance. She was the one who caused a revelation the others had either overlooked or weren't sufficiently interested in to bring out. She said to the Japanese, "You were here during the war, weren't you?"

He put down his cup, nodded his head several times, then studied Kathleen as he said, "Bad place here. Soldiers die because we can't get them back to Japan. I have charge of making the graves and keeping the records."

"Akira Yamamoto?" said Frank.

"Him too. Colonel's son. Very young then. Very hard on his father. No need for him to die here except that he got jungle rot and blood poisoning here. No way to get him off Emeraldia."

"You killed Colonel Yamamoto," said Dentzel, and the Jap smiled up at him without saying a word about that. He did, however, say something more to the point. "I spent two years in American prisoner camp on Okinawa. Learn English there. Learn other things."

Dentzel looked rueful. "Like where some gold bars were hidden on Emeraldia."

"No," hissed the prisoner. "I already knew about that. On Okinawa I learned how many bars were here — somewhere in this area —

182

and I remembered seeing Japanese flyers leave boxes behind on Emeraldia when they took back wounded soldiers."

"Boxes? That could have been medicine."

The look in the captive's eyes stopped Dentzel from saying what else could have been in the boxes. He nodded and the prisoner nodded back at him as though they had achieved understanding despite all barriers.

"What happened to the boxes?"

The Jap slowly shook his head back and forth. He did not know; he hadn't been interested at the time, except that armed guards had been posted for twenty-four hours he wouldn't have thought of it again. He said at the time all Japanese soldiers were terribly demoralised; that although their homeland kept beaming news of triumphs in the Pacific, the men in the actual theatre of war knew differently. It was a nightmare, he said, even in a place like Emeraldia where no one bombed them, because when the last airplane took off the last of the wounded, seventeen soldiers had to remain behind. He had been one of them.

He said they talked of killing themselves, of fighting the Americans when they should come until they were all killed, but in the end when Americans finally came to Emeraldia, the Japanese put out to sea in native boats trying to reach some other island, and were spotted by aerial observers who sent in fleet units to capture them. Afterwards, he went with the others to a prisoner-of-war centre on Okinawa, and that was where he heard stories of the lost loot, remembered seeing those heavily-guarded mysterious boxes, and later, after the war was over and he had been repatriated, he began to investigate quietly.

The man was very bland, very co-operative in everything. He was so helpful in fact that Alan finally said, "In case anyone is interested, our Nipponese friend here is keeping us standing around while time is working against us. The longer he can keep us immobilised the better the chances that his friends will find out what's happened."

Frank glanced at his watch. So did Dentzel and Courtland. Frank grimaced at the others; they had been very expertly taken in. The Jap smiled at Alan but the look in the black depths of his shiny eyes was far from amiable.

Alan had one more observation to make. "If we take him with us it's going to increase the risk. He only has to mislead us or yell out at the wrong moment. Leave him here with some of the older natives — the ones who were around when the island was occupied. Frank, you said you knew all the likely places. Do you think he'll help?"

Frank didn't think so. He said he'd get a couple of natives to watch the prisoner and Courtland provided his second surprise of the day; he produced a set of small steel chains ingeniously worked together to form passable handcuffs. "Picked them up as a curiosity in Haiti one time." He handed them to Carter who wordlessly stepped up and motioned for the captive to raise his wrists. The Jap hesitated, looked all around, then raised both hands. There was no other alternative.

Frank left the room and the others moved a little, some back towards the parlour, the Dentzels and Alan out as far as the pleasant coolness of the front veranda. Only Ford Courtland remained in the kitchen. He said to the prisoner in Japanese that murder was not a very pleasant thing to be punished for back in Japan. The prisoner agreed that it wasn't, but he added that there was no proof of murder.

Courtland was of the opinion that when all this was brought out, it would be a fairly simple matter for the Japanese authorities to prove what had happened to the wartime officers that had been stationed on Emeraldia. He then said, in English, "But if these people who have you now prefer charges for the murder of their Commissioner, my guess is that you'll wish you'd never done it."

"I didn't do it," the prisoner exclaimed quickly, also speaking English. "I didn't even know this man Friday was involved until he was killed, then I was told since he and Yamamoto were friendly, that he had been told of the hidden wealth, and had been disposed of to prevent him from telling others."

Courtland said thoughtfully, "Suppose I arranged for your escape. In exchange you tell me about the camp back in the bush."

The Jap widely smiled again. "You will find out about the camp, and I don't have to escape because you cannot prove I've done anything against the law."

Courtland turned as Frank and his shed-foreman, along with two other older natives, entered the kitchen. The Jap stopped smiling and for once Frank's foreman wasn't smiling either. The atmosphere of civilised consideration altered abruptly as Frank said, "There he is. Whatever happens don't let him get away. Do you understand?"

The foreman nodded, his companions stepped to chairs, and Courtland, looking at the prisoner, said, "I think you just made a bad mistake. *Sayonara.*" He and Frank went to where the others were waiting. They had wasted slightly more than an hour interrogating their prisoner but they probably had twice or perhaps three times that many hours left to find that camp and locate the radio which was on the same frequency as the radio of the Japanese fishing boat, which was somewhere over the horizon, out of sight.

CHAPTER NINETEEN

The Jap Camp!

Frank hadn't exaggerated, he knew the bush very well. When Kathleen asked how this happened to be, he smilingly said that for youngsters, particularly inquisitive ones such as he'd been as a child, Emeraldia was indeed a very small world. He'd explored every yard of the place, knew where every spring, each lagoon, all the grassy clearings were.

Herbert Dentzel and Courtland had rifles, the others had pistols, excepting Kathleen and she had no armament at all even though Courtland had offered her a small, light revolver.

Finding the trail their captive had used to leave his slight knoll behind Government House was no problem. Even when they encountered two other trails, each leading in a different direction, Frank unerringly chose the right one. It was, he pointed out, actually very elemental; the undergrowth showed definite indications of having been bent and broken by recent passages. He smiled. No, that wasn't how he did it at all, he was joking. He pointed southwesterly where the jungle got thicker, darker green, perpetually shadowed, and said there were only three clearings out there that had water. Each clearing was, in fact, a place where fresh-water had eroded tree roots, undergrowth, even the gorse-like dogged mangrove shrubs that could face sea-water with near impunity.

Anyone camping apart from everyone else on the island would need a clearing for his gear, of course, but most important of all in a place that turned humidly hot every day shortly before high noon and didn't cool off until the next pre-dawn, campers would need a convenient and palatable source of portable water.

There were only three springs in the jungle that could be used; Frank knew each one, its surrounding clearing, its distance and availability. He did not know which of the clearings would be the one they sought, but it had to be one of them, and they weren't so distant from one another searchers couldn't make the complete circuit with a minimal waste of time.

He didn't hasten. As he'd said at the bungalow, they were unlikely to encounter the other Japanese; they had ample time. He didn't even object to having Kathleen along although back at the village both he and Alan had protested that whatever ensued out in the bush was nothing for a woman to be involved in.

She had come anyway and it had to be confessed that striding along with her husband she was just as trail-wise and capable as any of the men. The fact that she'd refused to carry a weapon was offset by Courtland, striding along behind her who carried both rifle and belted pistol, and her husband who was similarly armed. Once, when they halted in a pleasant, cool place where speckled shadows camouflaged them all, she smiled at Alan and said she'd come to the conclusion that he was right, that living in the serenity of Emeraldia was very worthwhile. She pointed to the primeval place where they rested, pointed to dew-damp flowers, to the rotting stump of an ancient tree covered by flowering vines.

It was her husband who drily said, "Keep plenty of atabrin handy, and learn to like the same conversation from the same people three hundred and sixty-five days a year."

It was Ford Courtland who disputed that unflattering suggestion of what life would be like on Emeraldia. He said, "The answer is to have the best of both worlds, Mrs Dentzel, and the way to do that is to own a sea-going vessel so that when paradise palls, you can sail off to one of the larger islands where there are cities, and lose yourself in them for a week or so."

Carter and Bates seemed pained by this kind of talk but they said nothing; they simply made a long, careful study of the roundabout jungle then asked Frank how much farther to whichever destination he'd selected for their first goal.

Frank, watching Mrs Dentzel, shrugged at the sailors. "Half or three-quarters of a mile further along this pathway."

The blond sailor said, "Don't forget — there could be some kind of booby-trap up there."

Frank turned his head to steadily regard the blond man. "I won't forget, since I'm leading the group, Mister Carter, and have a positive abhorrence of being blown up from time to time."

They pushed on with Courtland and his seamen bringing up the rear, with Frank picking their route, with Alan, Dentzel and Kathleen in the middle of their small column.

Finally, they left the jungle behind, emerged into an area where the earth had to be more shallow, the underlying basic volcanic rock nearer the surface, because no large trees grew here and no bushes any taller than a man. Game trails were everywhere, as though every variety of predator who lived off the birds that inhabited this sunshiny place, used this treeless little expanse as a particular hunting ground.

Frank Chang halted on the far side of this shallow-soiled area and pointed through a thin stand of trees. There was a clearing through there. A sparkling brook not much wider than a man's stride, if that wide, cut across a grassy area that showed unmistakably that it was not inhabited by any species of living thing, two-legged or four-legged, that would otherwise have trampled down that lush grass.

Frank dropped his arm and turned to the others who were crowding up. "Dry run," he said laconically. "The odds were three-to-one; anyway, I'm just as glad this wasn't it because on the far side of this glade is a swamp which we'd have had to sneak through to make a circuit of the place." He turned without taking them any closer, glanced at his watch and struck out in a directly southward direction until forced to alter course upon the distant verge of the shallow-soiled place, by trees and jungle growth again. There, he took another trail. There too he increased the pace a bit. As he told Alan, who strode behind him now in single-file like the others because once again they were held to the pathway by huge, gloomy old trees festooned with dark vines, they were not pressed for time yet but on the other hand he didn't wish to have that happen until it was absolutely necessary.

The second clearing was smaller than the first and it was not preceded by inviting open places. The only warning the others had was when Frank rounded a bend and stopped dead still. On ahead through nearly impenetrable undergrowth was a great silent explosion of sunlight. All around was eternal gloom. The jungle was humid and dank enough to give an impression that clean sunlight hadn't touched the ground hereabouts for centuries — except for that open glade on ahead where the light was strong and dazzling.

Ford Courtland said it was an ideal place, that anyone needing privacy while at the same time wishing to be able to see in all directions, could probably not do as well anywhere else on the island. Frank nodded; that was true, he said, "And a little west by south of this place there is a low-tide lagoon where a boat could be brought in the day and throughout the night that little estuary would be dangerous for a vessel, but I suppose any boatman would realise that and stand away during those hours."

They pushed up into a little knot, standing close together because the trail was too narrow for anything else. Frank resisted the urgings of Courtland's two seamen to go any closer. He said it was highly probable this was their destination; if so, it could be foolish, even fatal, to push on down the trail to the clearing.

Courtland agreed. He was also of the opinion that they should have compelled their prisoner to reveal whatever it was on ahead that endangered them. He looked disapprovingly at Frank, who had prevented the captive from being subjected to Courtland's untender solicitations. Frank didn't even bother to acknowledge Courtland's temporary hostility. He pointed out to Alan where the trees intervened, between where they stood and the campsite. "My guess is some kind of warning device that operates either when it is stepped upon or disturbed by someone or something passing by or over it. Otherwise it'll have to be a device in the trees."

Alan agreed. "A simple sunlight beam directed from one mirror to another around the glade would work well."

"How?" Dentzel wanted to know.

"As long as the sunlight's heat is reflected off one mirror to maintain the heat upon another mirror, this kind of device cannot be triggered. But let someone walk between those mirrors, interrupt the heat-flow only for a moment, and the temperature drops which in turn activates a very simple switch. In this case I suppose an alarm bell might start ringing or perhaps some kind of explosive might be detonated. I would imagine the purpose of an explosive would be as much to alert the Japanese to the presence of intruders as it would be to injure someone."

Ford Courtland suggested that they fan out and make an inch-by-inch sweep towards the clearing. Kathleen was the first to baulk. "I wouldn't know a trip-wire if I saw one."

The seaman Bates nodded approval of this. "Maybe only a couple of us had better make the sweep. Otherwise sure as hell someone's goin' to set the thing off." He had been leaning against a black-trunked tree studying the onward jungle. "And there's something else too: Them Nips could be coming along behind us by now. I realise they aren't due for an hour or so yet, but there's no law says they couldn't knock off early. If they did that, then by now they also know their friend fell in a boar-trap and got captured." Bates grinned wickedly.

"I've had my share of skulkin' through island jungles after Nips and they're pretty good at that kind of thing. I'd suggest someone go back a ways and keep watch while we're tryin' to get into this camp."

It was all quite sensible. Frank and Alan were agreeable. So was Courtland who volunteered to go back and take up a position where he'd be able to detect pursuit. In the end though it was Herbert Dentzel who went back. He offered to do that because, when Frank asked who had experience with electronic devices, even home-made crude ones, Courtland had turned out, along with Fred Bates, to be qualified, while Dentzel confessed to knowing nothing about booby-traps of any kind.

Kathleen stood beside Alan watching her husband depart. He tried to be reassuring by saying that even if the Japanese came along, which wasn't too likely just yet, by the time they got close her husband would be too well hidden for them to detect him. She offered Alan a sweet smile and said nothing.

Courtland and Fred Bates pushed ahead, got clear of the others and began a painstakingly cautious advance towards the clearing. They did not call back and forth. With either hand-signals or simply an exchange of looks after they had separated in their gingerly-prosecuted search of the tangled jungle growth, they kept abreast of one another.

For Frank, Alan, the blond seaman Carter,

and Dentzel's wife Kathleen, it was an uncomfortable time. If Courtland or Bates tripped the warning device up ahead it could prove fatal to one or the other of them, perhaps even both of them, and it most certainly would warn the Japanese who were northeast of them, who could move very quickly to block their retreat. Alan lit a smoke, offered Frank and the others his pack, got no takers and said, "My guess is a combination of devices, one shoulder-high perhaps, the other across this path where it enters the clearing."

He was correct, at least as far as the trail was concerned. Fred Bates was stepping high and carefully through underbrush beside the path when he stopped very suddenly and emitted a soft, low whistle, that brought Courtland around. Bates pointed to the ground just ahead.

"Very good," he said in a soft tone that was clearly audible even as far back as where the stationary watchers stood. "Not original at all but damned well hidden." He stepped back into the path and beckoned the others to him.

They went carefully. When Bates raised a warning hand they stopped. He showed them the two sticks driven into the underbrush on each side of the only trail leading into the clearing. In the gloom of this place it was more difficult to make out the black, nearly invisible wire stretching between the wooden stakes.

Courtland leaned upon his rifle. There was a

dark sweat-stain down the back of his shirt starting between the shoulder-blades. He said in a gruff mutter, "I never liked this sort of thing. I prefer my enemies standing up in plain sight."

Bates dropped to one knee, studied the trip-wire carefully, turned and beckoned to Alan. "Take that other stake," he ordered, "while I take this one. Kneel there and put one hand on the stake, bear down very gently and for God's sake don't let up the pressure. Fine. Now then, Mister Chang, take this trip-wire loose from both stakes then all of you but Mister Barton go back round the bend in the trail."

Bates was smiling wickedly over at Alan. Until the wire had been removed and everyone had started moving back, Bates was silent. Then he said, "Mister Barton, one or the other of us is leaning on the triggering device of a landmine. If you faint now, and if it's under your stake, when the pressure let's up . . ." Barton rolled up his eyes.

CHAPTER TWENTY

The Secret Camp

Ford Courtland muttered something sharp to his seaman and Bates looked over his shoulder then looked back at Alan. He was still smiling, though, so whatever admonition Courtland had offered hadn't annoyed him. He said, "Mister Barton, there is a way to manage but I think that if you will simply keep the pressure on that stake with both hands and let me do the rest, we'll come out just fine."

Bates did not appear to slacken the pressure on his stake although he removed one hand very gingerly, keeping the pressure down hard with the other hand. He then began feeling the earth around the stake. Ford Courtland watched from back a short distance. Farther back, where the trail curved, the others stood peering. It was so quiet each bird call sounded inordinately loud.

Bates seemed to have knowledge of what he was doing. Fortunately for his purpose the ground was soft, because that enabled him to gouge into it gently with his fingers.

The mine, he eventually told the others in a calm tone of voice, was beneath his stick. All the same he cautioned Alan not to move, not to ease up any pressure, not to relax for a moment because there was a possibility another mine just might also be across the trail.

"One would be enough," he said, "but they may have planted another one, just for good measure."

The device was round, appeared to be made of some rough-cast variety of black iron, and in the centre where Bates placed two fingers where the sharpened stick had kept the detonator depressed, was the triggering mechanism. It was a simple thing; when the pressure was released a safety-catch was allowed to spring upright which in turn released a firing-pin. Bates plucked a twig, slipped it across the slots to hold the safety-catch down, lifted away the stake and sat back with both hands on his hips. He didn't look pale nor shaken although it was difficult to see how he managed not to after that harrowing experience. Eventually he rose, stepped over beside Alan, wordlessly dropped to his knees and bent to probe the ground.

There was no second landmine. Bates lit a cigarette with steady hands, rose to dust his knees and smiled at Alan. "Maybe I ought to tell you, I never did that before."

Alan stood up, the others came forward and Ford Courtland looked hard at his seaman. "You managed rather well for someone who never saw a landmine before."

Bates shook his head. "You misunderstood. I didn't say I'd never seen one before, I said I'd never disarmed one before. I was trained in demolitions in the army, but during peace-time we trained on duds."

Courtland looked at Alan, who was pale, and at Frank Chang who, with Kathleen, was gazing at the ugly black killing device. He stepped past on the trail peering forward. Frank walked over beside him, motioned for Bates to come up with him, then the pair of them resumed their way towards the golden-lighted clearing.

They were almost to the fringe when Kathleen stopped and said, "I think I'll sit down for a moment." The men gazed at her. Evidently she'd been hit by a delayed reaction and now her knees were turning rubbery. Alan said he'd stay with her. The others moved out again, stepping in silence over the trodden path, their anxious glances searching left and right, and on ahead.

Alan was tender. He offered her a smoke, which she declined, smilingly said if he'd thought he'd have brought along a wee drink. She smiled at him and sank down upon a great, smooth old stone.

"I'll be all right."

Alan looked back the way they'd come, which was also the way her husband had gone. He glanced at his watch and wondered if they could locate the radio, destroy it, and get away from this spot before the Japanese came along. He didn't mention this to Kathleen. Instead he said, "If anyone had told me when I first saw you that we'd be out here in the bush playing with landmines together, I'd have recommended he have his head examined. Still, if I have to risk being blown up with a companion, you'd be my first choice."

She appreciated his heavy humour, perhaps not for its sake, but perhaps rather because he was trying to be cheerful. She sighed, looked round, then raised her face to him. "I'm sorry about deceiving you, Alan. Maybe it wasn't necessary, but when Herbert and I first decided to come to Emeraldia we thought it would be best to provide ourselves with some kind of cover."

He nodded. "Understandable." He dropped down beside her. "My only regret was when I discovered that you were married."

She smiled at him. "With your share of seven million dollars you'll be able to forget."

They heard Courtland's flat, tough voice raised in enquiry up ahead in the clearing. Frank Chang answered. The words were indistinguishable but significant nonetheless. Kathleen suggested that the radio had been found. Alan hoped so. He didn't object to facing three Japanese, even if they were armed, but he said he didn't like the idea of having the ones out on the sea in the waiting boat rushing into the thick of things all armed and ready for mayhem.

Frank Chang appeared in the trail, beckoned and turned to gaze back towards the camp.

Alan asked if Kathleen were rested, she arose, nodded, and went along beside him towards the shadowy place where Frank waited.

The men beyond her sight, over in the sun-shiny clearing, were talking. Their voices sounded casual and clear. Frank looked at Kathleen enquiringly as she approached, and when she smiled to indicate she was quite all right, Frank said, "Well; it's the correct clearing and we've found everything but a radio-transmitter. Courtland is of the opinion they might take it along with them each day." He turned, pointed the way and led off back into the clearing where, the moment Alan and Kathleen stepped forth from the shielding pro-tection of giant trees, hot sunlight smote them, hard. It was well past the time of day when the heat came.

The Japanese encampment was very neat and orderly. There were cooking utensils, tools of several kinds, several metal lockers which no one had forced open yet and which Courtland thought probably held clothing and personal effects, and what appeared to be an airtight, water-tight food locker. Bates was in the act of opening this locker when Alan and Kathleen entered the area.

Courtland and his blond sailor were acting slightly annoyed and upset. It was understand-able. If the Japanese had their transmitting ap-paratus with them, and if they got a chance to use it before Dentzel or the others could get the thing away from them, what was now a rather simple local problem could very easily become something else.

Bates finished examining the food locker and strolled over where a little fresh-water spring seemed to come out of a flat rock. There, he found other food in tins which in order to keep the perishables cool and fresh, were partially immersed in the water.

Frank stood studying the camp, two parallel lines etched between his brows. He looked at his watch. It was getting along towards the time of day when anyone doing manual labour, even with such an incentive as those Japanese treasure-hunters had, would have to knock off because of the mounting heat and the de-energisingly high humidity.

"Forget the wireless," he said to the others. "They must have it with them. I think we'd better decide just what we're going to do next."

The unsmiling sailor said, "Lay an ambush back down that trail somewhere close to the spot where Mister Dentzel is keeping watch. What else can we do?"

No one answered the question although Ford Courtland seemed mildly piqued by the brusqueness of his sailor's statement.

Frank and Alan exchanged a look. Alan nodded. Without another word Frank turned and started away. He could walk briskly now since they'd traversed the path before and had removed the booby-trap. The last man out of the Japanese camp was Fred Bates. He'd found a wicker-encased bottle at the spring. It held *sake*. Bates had a long, thirsty pull on the bottle before tossing it back upon the moist ground and hastening after the others.

Up to this time, prior to finding the landmine and to a lesser extent afterwards as well, there had been an attitude of curiosity rather than of peril among the searchers, but perhaps as a result of Frank Chang's altered attitude as he led the way, or perhaps simply because they were now definitely moving towards some kind of confrontation with men they knew were killers, everyone seemed to change. They did not speak as easily nor as unguardedly as before. The men kept hands near weapons. Frank, out front, trod softly and kept his head moving. Kathleen, looking at Alan, found him as alert and changed as the others. She took her cue from that and kept silent as they moved back over familiar ground.

It was Kathleen's husband who finally halted the party by simply materialising out of half-light, half-dark shadows near what could have been a huge jacaranda bush except that it was flowerless and odourless. Dentzel asked about the camp. The others explained what had been discovered, emphasising what had *not* been discovered. He was interested, but as they stood talking in low tones Dentzel would occasionally turn with studied casualness and glance down the mottled, silent and ominously empty trail.

Finally he said, "I've been thinking. They're going to miss their friend and see that boar-pit."

Frank shook his head. "Not the boar-pit. I left orders for it to be filled in and smoothed over to erase all evidence. As for missing their friend, I wondered about that on the walk out here. It seems possible to me they might think he'd gone down to the village or had started back for their camp ahead of them."

"Not the village," argued Dentzel. "That's out. They obviously don't even want the natives to know there are any Japs about. Maybe they'll think he headed for camp. I certainly hope so."

Courtland had a suggestion. "The trail up ahead is straight. We should be able to conceal ourselves on both sides. I don't think we should wait too long. I'm beginning to get a feeling about losing our initiative if we don't get set for an ambush."

Dentzel was agreeable, but he had one point to raise. "Remember one thing; those Japanese are armed and deadly. If they killed Commissioner Friday as well as some other Japs in their homeland, don't think for a minute they're not going to figure the odds the moment they know we've waylaid them."

Courtland's impatience led him to say rather brusquely, "We know all this, Dentzel."

The answer from Dentzel came right back with a double-edged sound to it. "Then make up your minds to shoot to kill. That's exactly what those Japanese will do. They aren't going to surrender. Not if I know Japs." He reached, draped a powerful arm across Kathleen's shoulders and drew her to him near the flourishing pseudo-jacaranda bush. "Go hide," he said, and turned his back on the others, obviously indignant over Courtland's attitude.

Courtland would have spoken again but Frank raised a hand and threw the taller man a black scowl. Into that vacuum of silence Alan said, "Half on this side of the trail, half on the other side. Frank; you act as anchor-man. When they're between us and well up the trail, you sing out."

Frank emphatically shook his head. "Courtland speaks Japanese. Let him do it." Frank turned towards the lean, tough, older man. "Wait until you can see that they can't bust back down the trail, Mister Courtland. Never mind calling to us, we'll act on the sound of your voice. Call out in Japanese for those men to stand still, or whatever you think best. All right?"

Courtland nodded, his earlier annoyance with Herbert Dentzel beginning to also include Alan who had ignored him, as well as Frank Chang who was just giving him instructions as though he'd been a novice on his first perilous mission. Courtland turned, jerked his head at the unsmiling blond sailor and stepped out of the trail into the matting of spiny, prickly jungle growth.

Within moments the others had also faded from sight. There were a number of indications that men were moving through the shielding bush, then gradually all that movement stopped and except for some curious and distraught birds scolding from the interwoven tree limbs overhead, the jungle looked normal.

There was an endless variety of gnats, insects of every description, that lazily worked through and over and around the underbrush. Some could sting, some aimed for the eyes and ears, and a few, like ravenous mosquitos, made an annoying sound as they sought to stealthily drink someone's blood.

CHAPTER TWENTY-ONE

Ambush!

The reaction of those men — and the solitary woman — to a long humid, tense wait, was different; Fred Bates was bothered by a thirst which arose from the *sake* he'd drunk. He alternately squinted down the empty trail from his place of concealment, and wished to high heaven he'd brought along a canteen of cold water.

The Dentzels, sitting close together in a shield of impenetrable greenery, whispered a little now and then but did not move.

The two sailors were still and watchful. Of them all these two had perhaps least reason to consider the tenuous complications which had led to this time, this moment.

Alan and Frank were visible to one another but like everyone else, stared unwaveringly down the trail. If there had been a way to measure risk, to compare losses, to divine who stood to gain the least in terms of satisfaction, desires, comforts, it would probably have been clear that Frank Chang and Alan Barton could lose the most.

Courtland of course might also lose a lot. Since he'd professed only a lukewarm interest in the cache, had at one point been on the verge of chucking the whole thing, was already adequately successful, if anything happened to him now he could presumably call himself an utter fool. And yet, obviously Ford Courtland was a hard, perhaps even brutal, competitor; it was endemic in men who were hard competitors to accept challenges even though they could lose more than they could gain. It was the challenge. No one would ever deny Ford Courtland was a person to take up a challenge.

Each of them, silent and motionless in the speckled jungle, lying or crouching in wait like predators, had their private thoughts and it was entirely possible that the wait, the heat, the dank silence, worked like acid upon their inhibitions. When the Japanese appeared, unless they were prudent men, it was quite possible that they would die on that musty, shadowed little trail.

No one was sure the Japanese *would* appear. The fallacy in believing was based upon the Nipponese captive back in the village. Except for his disappearance the others would have come pacing along exactly as they'd been doing for weeks now, possibly even lulled towards a sense of security because they hadn't been interfered with in all that time.

But now one of their party had disappeared. There was a good chance they'd believe, as had been suggested, he'd come back to the camp ahead of the others. It was, in fact, the only hope, for if the Japanese didn't believe that, then any one of a number of unpleasant and unpredictable things might happen.

But they came.

It was the quick, tonal dips and rises, sometimes flat, sometimes fluting towards a surge of raspy decibels that announced their approach, and to each listener it was clear they were in argument long before any of them were visible. Some birds fled at their approach. These were the same birds that had scolded the ambushers but whose non-existent abilities to recall had permitted them to quite forget the ambushers were down there, once they were hidden and silent. Now, they squawked and sprang away from the approach of the newcomers.

The first Japanese was carrying a metal object resembling a suitcase. Obviously this was their wireless set. The man also had a digging tool over his shoulder. He was taller and heavier than the two men following him, and his attitude was of a leader. It was his harangue as they padded along that lashed the men behind him, but they seemed unconcerned. One had several tools in his hands.

The third Japanese carried a small, almost fragile-looking carbine with a long, curving cartridge magazine just forward of the trigger-guard. He seemed to be the only armed man among them, but this was simply because his weapon was visible while the loose, sweaty, somewhat baggy attire of his friends concealed pistols. He was smoking and as the tall one paused to turn and say something sharp, this shorter, more mongoloid-looking man's coarse lips split in a wide smile and he said something that must have angered the foremost man because he suddenly stopped, glared and seemed trying to make up his mind about something.

That was when Courtland, who had understood all this, stood up from the underbrush beside the trail, levelled his rifle and said something harsh in Japanese.

The men on the trail were stunned. Whatever their dispute had been about, it had engrossed their total attention. Even when they saw Frank Chang, Bates, Carter, Alan Barton, Herbert Dentzel, rise up on both sides of them, guns drawn and ready, they continued to stand there looking dumbly at Ford Courtland.

He gave them an order in Japanese. They did not obey it. He raised the rifle a little, snugged it back to his body and gave the same sing-song order a second time. That was when the man with the carbine turned only his head and saw the other guns, the other men behind him in the jungle. Without a word he dropped the carbine. He also spat out his cigarette for some reason he alone understood.

The leader of these men, both hands full, looked willing to make a scrap of it. The blond, cold-faced sailor discouraged him, perhaps less with his words than with the expression in his eyes. "You'd never come close to making it," he said softly, lowering the muzzle of his weapon to the tall Jap's middle. "You couldn't even drop the radio and shovel before I could blow holes in your belly. Just stand still. Real still."

It was excellent advice. Not very welcome perhaps, but sound. The second Japanese made a sigh that sounded more like a hiss, slumped in his tracks and looked at the ground, the common Oriental attitude of submission.

Dentzel blocked the onward path. Fred Bates blocked the rearward route. Men on both sides of the trail waited for the tall Japanese to make up his mind whether he proposed to die there or surrender there. He surrendered.

In very good English he said to Ford Courtland, "All right." He stooped to gently place the wireless case upon the ground. When he straightened back he said, "I knew this could happen."

Courtland smiled. "That's not what you told your friends; you said the one you had watching us was a drunk and a scoundrel."

The Japanese all peered at Courtland; it was unusual to find a Westerner who spoke or understood Nipponese, an extremely difficult language to use under any circumstances.

Courtland continued to thinly smile. "Your drunken friend is a prisoner in the village." He gestured with his gun. "Bates, Carter; search them. They'll have weapons under their clothes."

The search was accomplished in a professional manner. Courtland's pair of sailors left their own weapons on the ground so as to offer the Japanese no temptations. Courtland was proved correct; even the Jap with the carbine had a pistol under his sweaty jumper.

When their guns were taken any notions of resistance the prisoners might have had were very effectively curbed. Courtland then motioned the tall Jap away and went forth to pick up the metal-cased wireless. Dentzel came forward, Kathleen slightly behind him and looking very solemn, and also very pale.

"Turn," ordered Courtland. The Japanese obeyed. Frank Chang moved away warily, so did Fred Bates who had been barring the path towards Government House. The tall Jap studied Frank for a moment then spat out some word that only his companions and Ford Courtland understood. Frank looked up but Courtland didn't interpret. All he said was, "Don't worry about it; they had you pegged for half-Jap. They have a term for that." Courtland jerked his head. "Walk," he snapped at the Japanese, and added in their own language that they had better walk very slowly and remain in the centre of the path. It wasn't necessary to understand Courtland's words, his face, particularly his slitted, flattened mouth, told the real story. He wouldn't hesitate to kill.

Fred Bates kept off to one side of the short Jap who had been in the rear but who was now the leader of the captives. The captors moved into the trail too. It was a silent, wary procession, and although there were any number of places where a headlong dive might have permitted one of the prisoners to gain cover beside the trail, anyone with half an eye could imagine the results with all those armed men waiting, perhaps hoping, someone would do that.

When they came to the break, where the trail past the filled-in boar-trap lay, Courtland told his prisoners in their own language what had happened to the man they'd accused of deserting his post. The Japanese listened stoically and shuffled onward.

Just below Government House they encountered a dozen grinning natives with glistening coconut knives who obviously had been waiting in that place to watch this procession. How they had known what to expect was something they did not at this time bother to explain. They simply stood aside, smiling like wolves, watching as the Japanese went past, then they fell in behind the last man, Herbert Dentzel, and chattered happily as they trooped along.

In the village there was another crowd, only these people, among them Mama Kameha, neither smiled nor spoke. They merely stood in porch — and tree — shade watching. The younger ones were interested and curious, the older natives had long memories, it was they who showed nothing at all in their faces, but in their dark eyes was a smouldering glow of hatred.

The prisoners were taken to Frank's shed where the donkey-engine, cooling for an hour and more, stood upon its black, greasy foundation. Bates went to a waterbag and drank noisily. The others relaxed a little in the hot shade. The Japanese, with ample time for bitter reflection, did not look happy.

Frank sought his foreman and asked why he wasn't still with the other captive. The man grinned broadly. "No need. He drunk."

Everyone looked up. The dark face threatened to split wide open. "He wanted some *sake*. We found whiskey in your kitchen cupboard and gave him that. He drank it all. He fell off the chair."

Dentzel laughed. "Better than handcuffs anyway," he said. "I could use a drink myself."

Frank ignored that and told his foreman to fetch the unconscious prisoner to the paring-shed, then to clear the place of the natives. Throughout all this Kathleen, sitting on a small upturned box near the conveyor-belt, sipped water given her in a tin cup by her husband, while Alan and the two seamen slouched behind the prisoners. It was Mama Kameha who, having heard Frank's orders, turned to the crowd and said, "One beer on the house. Come along. It's all over here, anyway." She led the others in a dusty retreat, and finally the chatter began. Some of the things that were said were decidedly unflattering towards the captives; a few promises were made, of a grisly kind, if the

Japanese were to be set free on the island.

Courtland and the tall Japanese looked squarely at one another. Courtland, guessing the man's feelings, said, "Well; you could hardly expect them to feel otherwise, could you?"

The Japanese, gazing after the crowd, was silent. Whatever his thoughts, they were evidently just as uncomplimentary in context as were the statements of the natives.

Two men brought the unconscious Japanese. His companions, gazing upon the limp, reeking carcass, hissed disapproval which the captive blissfully ignored. Courtland removed the chain handcuffs, hooked them into his belt and, setting aside his rifle, looked squarely at the leader of the Japanese.

"Where is the gold?" he asked in English. The prisoner's flat, dark face twisted. His eyes shone with cold anger. He did not open his lips.

Courtland looked at Bates and Carter. They moved in closer, unsmiling, ham-fisted, physically powerful and willing men. Frank Chang interfered again as he'd done before under similar circumstances.

"Did you search the graves?" he asked, managing to get between the Jap and the two sailors, who stopped to await the answer to this question.

The Jap looked past Frank at the sailors, then dropped his eyes and studied Frank a moment.

But when someone spoke next it was one of the other Japanese. He said in painstaking English that they had searched the graves, the place where the hospital tents had been, they had even used steel probes to poke into the soggy soil for a quarter mile in all directions from that fateful site. They had found nothing.

This admission encouraged the other, heretofore quiet and dejected prisoner. He felt that if there had ever been a cache on Emeraldia, someone else must have found it long ago.

The tall Japanese finally looked straight at Courtland, who he seemed to believe was the leader of their captors, and said, "There is no bullion. There is no hidden wealth."

Dentzel smiled, lit a cigarette and very slowly shook his head at the tall Jap. "There's a cache somewhere," he said quietly. "You pulled a damn fool stunt, killing the men who knew where it was."

The Jap spat. "Liars!" he snarled. "They were liars!"

CHAPTER TWENTY-TWO

Paradise Lost

There was no problem getting guards to watch the prisoners while Frank, Alan, the Dentzels and Courtland went over to Frank's bungalow for something to eat. Bates and Carter remained behind, unwilling to trust the natives, or at least unwilling to trust them entirely. Frank took a native along to fetch food back for the seamen.

Later, when they were comfortably settled in Frank's parlour, Courtland said that although he'd been convinced the cache was on Emeraldia up until they'd interrogated the Japanese, now he was just as convinced that it was not.

Alan sided with Herbert Dentzel in believing they should take over the search from the Japanese and expand it. Like Dentzel again, Alan was satisfied the cache definitely was on Emeraldia.

It was inevitable that someone mention the difficulty the Japanese had encountered in their search, suggesting from this that someone had already found the wealth and taken it away. "What of those flyers who brought it here in the first place, back during the war, or those men who guarded it?"

It was of course a good point. Courtland said

if they made enquiries of their prisoners they'd doubtless discover that some of those Japanese were the same men who had either flown the bullion here or had, in fact, guarded it afterwards, "But," he continued, "that's not important nor germane. The puzzle of this cache is troublesome. Either it is still where they originally hid it and the jungle has changed so completely none of the original landmarks exist — or — among the men who were based here and who knew what was in those cases, one or more did surreptitiously return and dig the bullion up and take it away."

Frank spoke for the first time. "Not without a native knowing of it, Mister Courtland, but, for my part, I'd like to change the conversation for a moment to what is more important to me: What do we do with the prisoners?"

Courtland had an immediate solution. "Wireless Brisbane or Auckland — somewhere down there — for a corvette to sail up here, take them back and have them stand trial for murder. Commissioner Friday's murder."

Alan slowly shook his head. "Wireless Tokyo, Frank," he said, and did not enlarge upon that by so much as one word. He didn't have to, the implication was amply clear. If the prisoners were returned to their homeland to stand trial for the Japanese they had killed there, including the father of Akira Yamamoto, convictions would almost certainly be automatic, while punishment would be swift and harsh.

Frank started to say something to Alan when a light fist rapped upon the veranda door. He went across to open it while every head in the room followed his progress.

The caller was Mama Kameha. She had that band woven across the front of her hair to hold it in place which she only wore upon special occasions, such as the arrival of old Voermann's boat or the return of some islanders from 'working out'.

She said, "Frank; that drunk one is groaning and being sick down there at the sheds."

He nodded, eyeing her. "Thank you. I'll go down and look after him in a bit. Mama; you didn't come here tonight to tell me a Jap was sick-drunk."

"No."

"What then?"

"Well; I want you to promise me something first, Frank. Will you do that?"

"Probably, yes, but how would I know until I hear what I'm supposed to promise?"

"Promise me that you will never leave Emeraldia. Never go somewhere else to live."

Frank smiled. "Sure Mama, I promise."

"And Alan?"

"Do you want me to call him, he's inside?"

She nodded so Frank poked his head back through the door, caught Alan's attention and beckoned. The others, watching, were interested but since Frank made no move to include them they were free to assume this business

219

had nothing to do with them.

Alan stepped out onto the veranda, winked at Mama Kameha then listened to Frank's explanations. He then looked at Mama Kameha. "I wouldn't leave Emeraldia, Mama; I wouldn't have enough money to live anywhere else." He was being partially facetious so he grinned. She did not smile back at either of them.

"You got plenty," she said, almost truculently. "Frank; why'n hell you didn't tell me you were after that old Jap treasure!"

Frank slowly straightened up. Alan, in the act of fishing for a cigarette, stopped moving. They both fastened their eyes upon Mama Kameha. She was regarding them sternly. Frank whispered, "Mama; do you have it?"

"Sure," she said stoutly, unhesitatingly. "Sure I got it. Commissioner Friday and I dug it up three, four years ago."

Alan said, "Oh God," and put the cigarette packet away. "Where is it, Mama?"

"In the typhoon-shelter beneath my store." She looked back at Frank. "Since when you can't confide in me? How come you got to sneak round with all these outlanders instead of comin' to your real friends, Frank? I told you last night you weren't doing the . . ."

"Mama," interrupted Frank, "Please. How did you get that bullion into the cellar under your store, and are you sure it's all there?"

"Sure I'm sure it's all there. Commissioner Friday found it. You know how he was always poking around looking for something that might tell him how we native people first got on Emeraldia. He found it and the pair of us moved it. It took us a very long time. We could only work at night, and even then not every week did we get the chance. We started to hide it at Government House, but he said no, that someday someone would come looking for it, and they'd look in Government House first." Mama Kameha's round, amiable face turned ugly. "They came all right, didn't they — Japs! And they ain't changed at all. They killed him to find out where it was hid." Mama Kameha paused to savour a private thought and Frank, who knew her best, reached for her arm.

"They musn't kill them, Mama. We're going to see that justice is done. They'll be sent back to Japan for trial as murderers. I know how the natives feel but they musn't kill those Japs."

She didn't commit herself to this at all, but neither did she say openly she would oppose it. Instead she said, "Frank; if we let those people in your house have some of the bullion will they go away and stay away — particularly *that woman* — and will you and Alan keep your promises?"

Frank looked at Alan. "It's a mess," he murmured, and smiled. To Mama he said, "We can show them the bullion, Mama, but they can't have any of it. You see the wartime Japanese stole that bullion. We will have to call for an international tribunal of some kind to determine ownership of the cache's contents."

Mama looked surprised. "Ownership? Damned gold is heavy when you're carrying it on your back from up there down here in the night. *We* own it. Commissioner Friday told me that someday, when he could do so, he meant to use that money to make a fine stone wharf, build a school on Emeraldia, and do some other things for the islanders. It's our money, Frank."

"No, Mama, not unless the people it was stolen from say so. But I imagine we'll get a pretty substantial part of it as a fee for finding it."

"Finding it, Frank? Hell; it was never lost."

Frank smiled, put an arm round Mama Kameha's shoulders and said, "Alan; the others have to hear this."

The others did hear it — in stunned silence. When Mama Kameha had told it all, in her own unabashed way, Ford Courtland eyed her with a twinkle. He wasn't viewing her as she now was, standing before them waiting, looking, not liking any of them very much because they were aliens but tolerant in her way, honest, sincere and amiable. The way Courtland viewed her was different. What had Mama Kameha looked like twenty-five, thirty years ago when she'd been in her prime, full bodied, high-breasted, with golden skin and perfect white teeth — what had she been like when Alfred Harold Frederick Friday had come to Emeraldia, last colonial administrator, a single man, impressionable, in love with paradise before he even set foot in it. He had been Ford Courtland's uncle. As different as they may have been, they were not all *that* different. Courtland arose, gently smiling.

"May we see it, Mama?" he asked.

She looked at Frank, at Alan, then over at the only other woman in the place. "Sure. It's dirty; it's been down there ever since Mister Friday and I put it there."

Herbert Dentzel laughed. "Dirty gold bars."

Mama looked again at Frank and Alan, as though she weren't altogether certain this was the right thing. They nodded at her. So did Courtland who, as they walked out into the settling night, paused a moment to look at the enamel sky, the quiet, whispering surf, the trees and sheds and the shimmering bay where his *Eleuthera* rode lazily at anchor. He said, "Mama, what did Mister Friday have in mind when he moved that gold?"

"A school here, a fine stone wharf, a new wireless."

Ford Courtland smiled and said nothing as they all descended the steps to the warm and dusty roadway and started towards Mama Kameha's building. In passing near the shed where the Japanese were being held Frank acknowledged the broad grin of his shed-foreman who leaned upon an upright-post with his shiny machete in one fist. The prisoners were hunched and silent, moving just their faces to watch Mama Kameha lead their captors on past and towards the centre of the village.

Kathleen left her husband's side and pushed ahead. Mama Kameha looked at her, and smiled. They were up ahead of the men, who were beginning to offer their thoughts to one another. Mama Kameha said, "You know how to love a man, huh?"

Kathleen nodded. "You loved him . . . ?"

"Oh yes. He was *good*. Do you know?"

Kathleen smiled but this time she did not nod. She simply said, "Different women want different things in men. Tell me how he was good, Mama, because someday I'd like to write a book about him."

"That would be very nice. He was kind to people. And he understood exactly. When the missionaries came, he understood. Well; I can't tell you except to say he was a very wise and gentle man."

"And you loved him."

Mama paused out front of her building and turned. "Frank; you know how to get into the cellar. You take them down there. The girl and I will wait out here."

Frank nodded and led the way on past but Dentzel touched his wife's arm in passing and said, "Aren't you coming, love; have you any idea . . . This will be the only time in your lifetime you'll ever see seven million dollars worth of gold bars."

Kathleen, with Alan's and Frank's eyes upon her, smiled at her husband. "You look, then you can tell me. I think I'll wait."

The men trooped past. There were a number of natives loitering on the veranda. As though they didn't exist Mama Kameha planted herself upon one of the wide steps leading on up, patted the scuffed planking at her side and when Kathleen sat down Mama said, "Now I'll tell you something because you want to know about him. You like Frank?"

Kathleen, not following this, said cautiously, "Mister Chang? Yes, I like him."

"Well; the Commissioner sent Frank's father away." Mama looked into Kathleen's face. "He gave him some money, told him never to come back, and sent him away."

"But why?"

"He was no good. Mister Friday believed in love. Frank's father didn't believe in love. He believed in getting people — girls — drunk. He was no good." Mama patted Kathleen's hand. "Well; you wanted to know about him, so I'm telling you."

"Mama; tell me about *you* and the Commissioner."

The round face softened, the still-perfect teeth shone, the tawny eyes reflected moonlight on the bay. "No, I couldn't tell you that. You know how long we loved? More than twenty years. That is about as long as it can be so with people, isn't it? He said many times as long as

225

he lived he would keep civilisation away from Emeraldia, and he did it. But now he is gone . . ."

"You have Frank and Alan."

Mama nodded. "For how long? They are young men. I saw how they both looked at you."

"But I've seen some exquisite native girls, Mama."

"Maybe. I don't know, maybe it will work out like that. I pray for that, but I think something else too."

"What?"

"That gold."

"Mama, you heard what Frank said. An international tribunal will take it over."

"Mister Friday said many times gold is poison. Just the ground it touches is poisoned. Wherever it has been is never the same again. The newspapers will print all this, people will come here who never heard of Emeraldia before. There will be many among them like Frank's father. Mister Friday used to say something — he used to say a man named Milton was right, that paradise was indeed lost." Mama looked at Kathleen as though doubtful what Mama didn't understand herself, might also not be understood by the lovely girl at her side.

Kathleen understood. She took Mama Kameha's hand in both hers and held it tightly a moment, then released it.

When the men returned, oddly silent, Kathleen saw how each of them had been subtly changed just by looking at something. She had a lump in her throat because she knew exactly what Commissioner Friday had meant. Paradise was indeed lost, and his murder had been the first wickedness leading down to that loss.

The employees of G.K. Hall hope you have enjoyed this Large Print book. All our Large Print titles are designed for easy reading, and all our books are made to last. Other G.K. Hall books are available at your library, through selected bookstores, or directly from us.

For information about titles, please call:

(800) 223-2336

To share your comments, please write:

Publisher
G.K. Hall & Co.
P.O. Box 159
Thorndike, ME 04986

P